Forgotten Heroes
of the
North East

by Mike Gibb

BY THE SAME WRITER

Plays & Musical Plays

A Land Fit For Heroes

Mother of All the Peoples

Five Pound & Twa Bairns

Sunday Mornings on Dundee Law

Clarinda

Red Harlaw

Aberdeen's Forgotten Diva

Outlander the Musical

As Long as But a Hundred of Us

Scatter My Ashes On Mormond Hill

Children of the Sea

Lest We Forget

Doorways in Drumorty

Giacomo & Glover

Books

It's A Dawgs Life

Waiting For the Master

Ask Anna

How To Train Your Owner

Anna's Adventures In Wonderland

When Angus Met Donny

Sammy the Tammy (The Mystery of the Missing Mascot)

The Name's Sammy, Sammy the Tammy

Drumorty Revisited

Forgotten Heroines of the North East

A Stepping Stone to Stardom

Heroes of the Halbeath Road

Just Another Seterday in Dundee

This book is dedicated to Norma who has been my greatest supporter
and best friend for more years than I could possibly deserve

Acknowledgements

Grateful thanks are owed to many people for their assistance with this book:

To David Stout of Sketchpad for designing the cover and helping with the layout.

To Patsy Davidson, Bill Gibb's sister, for providing a wealth of information, drawings and photographs.

To Dame Twiggy Lawson for contributing an original piece about her memories of Bill.

To Isobel Gregory for photographs of Bill Gibb's school days and Shane Strachan for information on his Bill Gibb Line exhibition and film.

To Chris Reid at Fraserburgh Heritage Centre for details about several of the Forgotten Heroes.

To Bob Watt from Rosehearty for invaluable help in researching the life of Hugh Mercer and his granddaughter Rebecca Watt for the lovely drawing on page 19.

To Anne Malcolm of the Thomas Blake Glover Foundation for invaluable assistance and advice and for helping source photographs courtesy of Nagasaki City Library 'Glover Albums'.

To Lorraine Noble for information on several Fraserburgh born figures in particular James Ramsay.

To Carolyn Johnston of VSA for flagging up the work of Provost Alexander Nicol and the VSA for use of photographs in the appropriate chapter.

To my faithful proof readers Heather McBride, Norma Gibb and Michael Craig..

Hugh Mercer (1726 – 1777)

From the Buchan shore to Moon River

What do famous Second World War General George Patton and prolific Tin Pan Alley song writer Johnny Mercer have in common? The obvious answer is that they were both American but there is a far more important and interesting connection than that. They are, in fact, both direct descendants of a man born in Pitsligo, Aberdeenshire.

Pitsligo is a parish four miles from Fraserburgh comprising of Rosehearty, Peathill and, at one time, Sandhaven. Pitsligo also boasted a Castle of the same name, the ancestral seat of Lord Forbes of Pitsligo and more than one Church. And it was in the manse adjacent to one of these, the Pitsligo Kirk, that on 16 January 1726 a son named Hugh was born to Church of Scotland minister the Reverend William Mercer, who served as a preacher for a remarkable 47 years, and his wife Ann.

Most children born into such a rural environment would have left school at an early age to work on a farm or undertake similar menial work before marrying some local lass, probably called Jean, and producing a brood of children. But Hugh Mercer was clearly not like most of his contemporaries as by age fifteen he had been accepted into Aberdeen University to study medicine.

Four years later Hugh emerged from Marischal College with a degree in medicine and, had it not been for events that had occurred more than fifty years earlier, would probably have returned home, married someone called Jean and set up in country practice. But circumstances dictated that was not the road he was to follow.

Back in November 1688 the ruling Catholic Monarch, James II (James VII of Scotland), suddenly realised that the Stuart household wouldn't be playing 'Happy Families' that Christmas as he was suddenly deposed by his daughter Mary and her Protestant husband, the Dutchman William of Orange, in what became known as the Glorious Revolution, a title that James would have clearly disputed. The overthrown Monarch headed for exile in France where he largely lived out his days. The Stuart dynasty had a long and illustrious lineage in Scotland and this turn of events was not well received, especially in the Highlands and the North East, and resulted in the formation of the Jacobite movement, the name being derived from the Latin word Jacobus meaning James.

James Francis Edward Stuart was only five months old when his father was sent packing and the young boy was brought up in France. Throughout his life, no doubt encouraged by those who dreamt of the Royal house of Stuart being restored, he plotted and planned to take back the throne. In 1715 James, who became known as 'The Old Pretender', was buoyed up by news of Jacobite uprisings in Scotland and Cornwall and although both of those petered out he decided to return to claim the throne of the country he had left as a babe in arms. He departed France in the depths of winter but took ill while at sea, developing a fever. Bearing in mind that it was December he might have been wise to turn the ship around and head for the likes of the Bahamas but instead he battled on to Peterhead of all places; not an ideal spot at that time of year if you are feeling a little off colour. It was a particularly harsh winter and by January he opted to head for the slightly more clement climes of Scone Palace in Perthshire. While there he learned that Government forces were heading his way and quickly scuttled off to Montrose to board a ship to take him back to France, leaving behind his loyal, if somewhat disillusioned, followers. It is fair to say that the 1715 is unlikely to feature on any Google list of the 'Ten Best Rebellions'.

That might have been the end of the Jacobite cause had it not been for his son, the Young Pretender or Charles Edward Stuart, who thirty years later decided to follow his father's example and come to Scotland with regal intentions. He was initially a great deal more successful than Papa had been and following victory on the battlefield of Prestonpans and the capturing of Edinburgh, a decision was made to invade England. The Jacobite army marched south largely unimpeded reaching Derby where word filtered through to the effect that Londoners, and especially the members of the ruling Royal Family, were quaking in their collective boots, convinced that the northern hordes were heading their way.

But Bonnie Prince Charlie's Generals developed 'pieds froids', or in Scottish terms 'cauld feet', and instead of marching on the capital retreated north in the hope that more people from England and France would swell their numbers. Despite a success at Falkirk the rebellion was losing momentum with the Jacobite soldiers tired and hungry and weary. The end came on 16 April 1746 on a barren moor at Culloden near Inverness.

Lord Forbes of Pitsligo was a staunch supporter of the Jacobite cause and had rallied to the Old Pretender's call in 1715. When he heard that Charlie Edward Stuart was coming to Scotland Forbes raised a small army of about 100 from the Fraserburgh area which he himself led despite his advancing years and infirmity and set off to join the young Prince. And amongst that assembly was Hugh Mercer who acted as surgeon to the Jacobite troops at that last stand at Culloden.

There is a popular misconception that the battle on Culloden Moor was a Scotland v. England affair but in truth the Government force that the Jacobites faced was a mixture of English soldiers and Lowland Scots opposed to the Stuarts while other Lowland Scots and French and even a sprinkling of English soldiers fought with Charlie. Outnumbered and poorly equipped Charlie's motley band was routed and an estimated 1500 of them were killed with a further substantial number captured. The rest fled for their lives with their leader being smuggled to Skye dressed in women's clothes (long before it became popular) before subsequently returning to France.

The aftermath was nothing short of barbaric. Under the leadership of the Duke of Cumberland, or Butcher Cumberland as he became known, the Government forces slaughtered wounded men on the field of battle or stripped them and left them naked to die from exposure. Local men, women and even children thought to be sympathisers or even seen clothed in tartan were indiscriminately murdered with females also suffering rape. Laws were quickly brought in to make wearing kilts illegal, subject to a six months jail sentence, and the playing of bagpipes and the speaking of Gaelic were both banned. Jacobites that had escaped were hunted down and captured with many being executed and others transported.

Lord Forbes went into hiding, spending a considerable time dressed as a beggar and living in a cave near Rosehearty and in a barn at Holland Park. There was a huge reward offered for his capture but he was so well thought of by the locals that none would betray him. Like so many other Noblemen his property was confiscated and the seat of Pitsligo Castle fell into disrepair and is now a ruin. While in hiding Forbes adopted the pseudonym of a Sanny Broon and messages from Jacobite sympathisers still at large were delivered to him by a well known local worthy by the name of Jamie Fleeman.

Fleeman was born in Longside in 1713 and was a strange looking man with a large head, huge shoulders and unruly hair who provoked fun amongst his contemporaries. He travelled around the North East dressed in little more than rags and always barefoot and after he went to work for the Laird of Udny at Knockhall Castle he became known far and wide as the 'Laird o' Udny's feel'. In truth that title was earned through his wit and his ability to act as a court jester rather than through any simple mindedness. One of his most famous exchanges was when he was stopped on the road by a well-to-do gentleman who demanded to know who Jamie was and was met with the response 'I'm the Laird o' Udny's feel. Fa's feel are you?'

Fleeman became famous throughout the area when a fire broke out in Knockhall Castle while everyone was asleep and Jamie was awakened by the barking of the dog that was his constant companion. Using super human strength that his somewhat strange body shape gave him he threw an enormous oak chest through a window thereby providing an escape route before rousing the Laird and his family and leading them to safety. However he didn't bother wakening anyone that he didn't care for and it was only after the pleading of others that he returned to the burning building to rescue a domestic servant with whom he had a disagreeable relationship.

JAMIE FLEEMAN.

The Laird and his 'feel' thereafter moved to Udny Castle and during his stay there he became friendly with the Countess of Erroll, a fervent Jacobite, who used Jamie to transport messages to supporters including Lord Forbes in his cave hideout as she endeavoured to garner support for the failing cause. Fleeman's death came in some sad circumstances. In 1778 he was caught in very heavy rain and soaked so badly that he developed a fever. Refused shelter by a number of people he wandered around before falling asleep in a barn.

When someone tried to enter Fleeman was hit on the head by a large plank of wood causing a serious injury. Despite his weakened condition he managed to walk eight miles to his sister home where he passed away two days later.

A memorial to Jamie Fleeman was erected at his grave in Longside in 1851 but even that wasn't the end of the story as he is referred to by Bram Stoker in his book 'Dracula's Guest and Other weird Stories' while a character in Sir Walter Scott's novel 'Waverley' is believed to be based on the Laird o' Udny's feel.

Like Lord Forbes, Hugh Mercer also became a fugitive taking refuge wherever he could find it, principally in a farm in his native North East, until a year after Culloden when he was eventually able to secure a berth on a ship leaving from Leith and heading for the New World. While at sea the ship's captain took ill and was nursed back to health by Mercer; as a thank you part of his passage fee was refunded to him. Mercer arrived in Pennsylvania but on realising that he had left one country under the heel of the British only to land in another he felt that it would be unwise to linger. Being a wanted man for his support of the Jacobite cause he decided that somewhere off the beaten track would be a safer bet and headed with a wagon train for the predominately Scottish/Irish community of Conococheague, named by the local Delaware Indian tribe for the stream nearby and meaning 'many turns river'.

He settled in Franklin County, Pennsylvania in a small settlement (now called Mercersburg in his honour) and for the next eight years tended the sick in that area. It was not an easy life as the settlement and its inhabitants were frequently the victims of attack by the natives and Mercer regularly had to attend to injuries caused by arrows, spears and tomahawks, problems he had never encountered in Pitsligo.

At that time America was largely under the rule of the British and the French and once again a dispute between these near neighbours, albeit over land thousands of miles away, erupted and descended into what became known as the Seven Year War. Both sides were supported by recruits from Native Indian tribes and battles were bloody and vicious as was clearly displayed when the British attacked the French strong hold of Ford Duquesne in Pennsylvania (now the site of modern day Pittsburgh) close to where Mercer was living but were heavily defeated in the process.

Mercer was appalled by the barbaric manner in which the defending army dealt with the British forces and it brought back horrifying memories of the butchery displayed on that Highland field. He offered his services to tend to the wounded and the dying and weeks later found himself joining the British army despite the fact that less than a decade earlier he had been fleeing from them fearing for his life. He laid down his medical equipment and picked up a musket, being appointed Captain Mercer. It was not a particularly wise choice of career as within a year he was severely injured during an attack on an Indian camp and spent ten days trekking a hundred miles through forest land in great pain, existing on a diet of berries, clams and rattlesnake before stumbling into Fort Shirley only to discover that it had been deserted by the army. After a couple of days of rest and recuperation, enjoying considerably more palatable food provided by volunteer rangers, he set off again for Forty Lyttelton where he was warmly greeted. For his heroics he was promoted to Colonel serving alongside a man who would become his lifelong friend. A gentleman called George Washington who many years later was elected as the first President of the United States but at that time was merely a serving officer in the British Army. George Washington is also remembered as the President who never told a lie which makes him somewhat the polar opposite of the President who most recently vacated the Oval Office.

When the British and French eventually settled their differences and the war finally ended Mercer relocated to Fredericksburg in Virginia attracted by the fact that it had a thriving Scottish community and returned to medical matters. Having bought land in the area Mercer put down roots and joined the local Masonic club which later became a hot bed for supporters of the American Independence movement providing a substantial number of officers for the Revolutionary Army including his old pal Washington.

Settled in Virginia Mercer established a doctor's surgery and apothecary tending to the local populace with one of his distinguished patients being Mary Washington, his great friend's mother. He bought Ferry Farm from George Washington and married local girl Isabella Gordon who bore five children, four boys and girl. Mercer was clearly hoping to settle and live out his life in tranquillity; sadly there was to be no peace in that valley.

General George Washington

In 1770 America comprised of 13 colonies all governed from London. The British Government, having spent huge sums on the war with the French, was in financial difficulties and decided to try to balance the books by imposing new taxes, including the hugely unpopular Stamp Act, on their Colonial cousins. These actions caused great resentment and led to unrest including the infamous Boston Tea Party which, despite its name, did not involve an afternoon of sharing scones and a cuppa but rather the boarding of British vessels in Boston harbour before throwing its cargo of chests of tea, a very valuable commodity back in 1773, into the water.

Matters escalated and by 1775 when full scale conflict had broken out the locals in twelve of the colonies formed a Continental Congress with an Army under the leadership of General George Washington. Clearly King George III was in no mood to surrender power and sent British troops augmented by mercenaries including crack German troops called the Hessians. The somewhat rag tag Continental forces were no match for these highly trained fighters and in the months after the Colonies issued a Declaration of Independence on 4 July 1776, they suffered one defeat after another with their initial 20,000 men being decimated by fatalities, captures, ill heath and desertion.

By the time that Christmas 1776 approached Washington had retreated and made camp with the remnants of his army, many suffering from dysentery, near starvation and devoid of winter clothing, on the south bank of the Delaware River safe there only until the pursuing British forces were able to cross the waterway when it froze over. And amongst the small band of loyal followers was a certain gentleman from Aberdeenshire now known as General Hugh Mercer.

While living a peaceful life in Fredericksburg Mercer had, like many of his contemporaries, voiced his displeasure at the actions of the British Government in London but was initially prevented from playing any active role as he was viewed as being a 'Northern Briton', a great insult for a proud Scot. Months later, however, in early 1776 he was appointed Colonel of the 3rd Virginia Regiment and was summoned to New York. Despite the frequent reversals that the Continental Army suffered during the initial weeks of the conflict Mercer could claim one of the few successes.

He led his men in an attack on Richmondtown, Staten Island, capturing the town only for it to be retaken by superior British forces days later with Mercer and his troops having to flee to New Jersey where he was reunited with mentor George Washington and joined him in the retreat south.

As Christmas Day 1776 approached Washington was facing the fact that the armed insurrection was in danger of falling apart. Not only were the troops weary, cold, in ill health and short of all essential supplies many had only enlisted until the end of the year and it was clear from the general mood in the camp that they wouldn't be hanging around once they were legally able to leave. Washington knew that something had to be done to improve the morale of the men who spent day after day sheltering in flimsy tents during the cruel Pennsylvania winter. But what?

History suggests that it was Washington who came up with an audacious plan but in some quarters credit for the idea is attributed to Hugh Mercer. What is not in dispute is that what was to follow was the turning point of the American Revolutionary War. Twelve hundred Hessian troops had established a base on the other side of the Delaware in the small town of Trenton, New Jersey, no doubt waiting in relative comfort for the river to freeze over so they could mount an attack.

The Hessians were formidable opponents and, not surprisingly, Washington's men were terrified of them. It was clear that it would be madness to consider facing them in a conventional manner and that was when the plan was hatched. It was known that the Germans would celebrate Christmas in an exuberant manner with an abundance of food, and more importantly, drink and so on Christmas night while the Germans celebrated, the Colonial Army weren't to be found crowded round their camp fires singing carols but instead were climbing aboard a number of small boats commandeered from a nearby foundry to cross the icy and dangerous Delaware River.

It took some ten hours to ferry an estimated two thousand four hundred men across, with many more having to be left behind because of time restraints, and the soldiers then faced a nine mile march in darkness through forests before reaching Trenton. Washington and Mercer had hoped that they would complete the trek before dawn but it took longer than expected and they arrived in daylight. Fortunately, however, the festivities of the previous day had had the desired effect and the Hessians were still sleeping off the excesses of a very Merry Christmas day when the Continentals descended on them.

What followed can't really be described as a battle as it was far too one sided for that. A small number of Hessians died in the skirmish, including their formidable and legendary leader Colonel Johann Rall, while others ran away but the invading force captured nine hundred of the German troops without suffering a single fatality in the process. It was a huge fillip for Washington and his men as well as providing them with warm clothing, food and much needed arms and other equipment.

It was undoubtedly a major moment in the armed struggle although the war continued for another seven years before the Treaty of Paris brought peace and saw the Colonies finally enjoying the Independence they had declared so boldly in 1776. Sadly Hugh Mercer, a man who had given so much to the cause, never saw that historic moment.

Less than two weeks after he had enjoyed the great victory at Trenton, Mercer was leading a brigade of soldiers near Princeton, New Jersey when they encountered two British regiments and a fight broke out. Mistaking the leader of the Colonial Army for General Washington they surrounded Mercer and ordered him to surrender. He refused to do so and drew his sabre but heavily outnumbered he was bayoneted seven times and left for dead. Becoming aware of the difficulties being encountered by his friend Washington rallied the men and drove the British back before defeating them in Princeton. As a consequence of this victory a large number of the men re-enlisted and the Colonial Army flourished.

Hugh Mercer was taken to a nearby field hospital but despite the best efforts of the surgeon he died nine days later on 12 January 1777 and was buried in Laurel Hill Cemetery in Philadelphia. Gone but certainly not forgotten. Artist John Turnbull painted *The Death of General Mercer at the Battle of Princeton* with the son of the slain war hero, Hugh Mercer Jr., posing as his father for the portrait while another well known painting *Washington at the Battle of Princeton* by Charles Wilson Peale shows Mercer lying mortally wounded.

General Mercer being carried from the battlefield at Princeton

But Mercer is remembered in other ways and in far more recent times. The events of Trenton produced a feature film called *The Crossing* with Jeff Daniels playing George Washington and Roger Rees in the role of Hugh Mercer. Another future American President Alexander Hamilton was also at Trenton and has since gone on to be immortalised in the hit musical *Hamilton* the score including a song titled 'The Room Where It Happens' with the lyric *"Did ya hear the news about good old General Mercer? You know Clermont Street? They renamed it after him. The Mercer legacy is secure."* In fact that was far from the only street named after Mercer while there are seven Counties stretching from New Jersey to Missouri, several towns and the school in Fredericksburg all boasting the name of the valiant Scotsman who gave his life for his adopted country. A remarkable testament to a young loon from Pitsligo.

Roger Rees (centre) as General Hugh Mercer in *The Crossing*

But there is great deal more to the legacy of Hugh Mercer than just places being named in his honour. His daughter Ann Gordon Mercer married a fellow Scottish immigrant Robert Patton and Ann gave birth to a son named John Mercer Patton who went on to distinguish himself in many walks of life, including physician, lawyer and judge, before being elected to the US Congress. He had a family of seven including five sons all of whom followed in their Grandfather's footsteps as military officers.

All wars are evil but surely there can be nothing quite as insidious and malevolent as a Civil War which can, literally, pit brother against brother. Less than eighty years after the American colonies had won their independence and formed the Confederate States of America, there being 34 States by the mid 19th Century, conflict had broken out again. Most wars result from a myriad of reasons although look closely and the sticky fingers of political power can usually be detected. The American Civil War was, however, mainly the result of one thing only; King Cotton. The economy of the Southern States relied heavily on the production and sale of cotton and the cotton was primarily picked by unpaid labour. Slaves.

The war broke out in April 1861, a month after Abraham Lincoln had become the 16th President, and one of Lincoln's key policies was the abolition of slavery, a practice which he considered abhorrent. Terrified by the prospect of losing their free labour seven of the Southern states seceded from the Union and displayed their determination to establish their own Confederation by attacking Fort Sumter in the harbour of Charleston, South Carolina, a city with a strong link to slavery; the market through which thousands of enslaved Africans passed over the years has been retained as a somewhat grotesque museum.

The conflict raged on for four long and bloody years before it was eventually brought to an end in April 1865 when General Robert E. Lee surrendered although it was two months later before the final Southern soldiers laid down their arms and accepted defeat.

President Lincoln had achieved his dream of abolishing slavery although he wasn't able to enjoy his success for long. A mere six days after Lee had surrendered to Union General Ulysses S. Grant, Lincoln

Descendants of Hugh Mercer

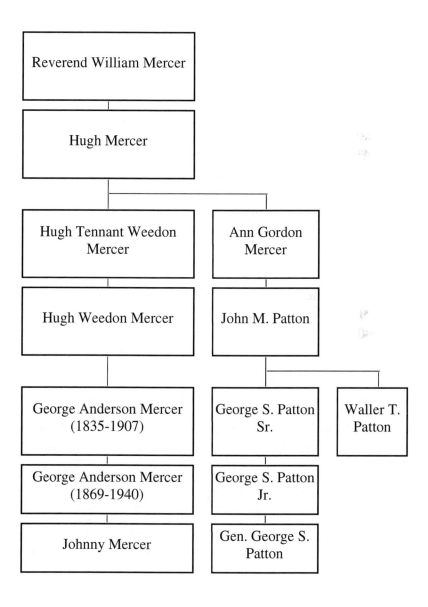

attended the Ford Theatre in downtown Washington D.C. to watch the play *Our American Cousin,* sitting in a box with friends. At 10.15 on the evening of 14 April 1865 John Wilkes Booth, a Confederate sympathiser and failed actor, crept into the box and shot Lincoln in the back of the head. Although Booth escaped he was tracked down and killed two days later.

Lincoln was taken in a coma to the Petersen House nearby but never regained consciousness, dying early the following morning just another casualty of a war that cost 620,000 lives, a death toll that is only fractionally less than the combined total of fatalities of all other wars (two World Wars, Korea, Vietnam, Afghanistan, Iraq and others) that America has participated in. Lincoln was immediately succeeded by a President Johnson just as, somewhat curiously, another assassinated President John. F. Kennedy was almost a hundred years later.

Among that horrendous death toll of over six hundred thousand souls were two of the five sons of John Mercer Patton, George and Walter. It was a tragic loss but nothing compared to that suffered by a lady called Mrs. Lydia Bixby from Massachusetts who also had five sons engaged in the war albeit on the Union side. Not one of them returned. On learning of this President Lincoln was so moved that he wrote a personal letter to the lady.

I have been shown in the files of the War Department a statement of the Adjutant General of Massachusetts that you are the mother of five sons who have died gloriously on the field of battle. I feel how weak and fruitless must be any words of mine which should attempt to beguile you from the grief of a loss so overwhelming. But I cannot refrain from tendering to you the consolation that may be found in the thanks of the Republic they died to save. I pray that our Heavenly Father may assuage the anguish of your bereavement and leave you only the cherished memory of the loved and lost and the solemn pride that must be yours to have laid so costly a sacrifice upon the altar of freedom.

George S. Patton, great grandson of the lad from Pitsligo, served as a Colonel in the 22nd Virginia Infantry and was killed, aged 31, at the Battle of Opeqon, having twice been wounded in early skirmishes. He was buried alongside his brother Walter, who perished at Gettysburg, in Mt. Hebron Cemetery. George left behind four children, the eldest also called George, graduated from the Virginia Military School but, rather sensibly, decided to shun army life and followed a law career, becoming an Attorney in Los Angeles before being elected as the first Mayor of San Marino.

Confederate General George S. Patton

But although that man may have shied away from a military life the same could certainly not be said about his own son, yet another George S. Patton, better known by the nickname 'Old Blood and Guts'.

To describe General George Patton as larger than life would be a massive understatement and legendary would be a far more accurate epithet. Patton was born in San Gabriel, California on 11 November 1885 and by age 17 was off to the Virginia Military Institute following in the footsteps of his father and grandfather. He subsequently graduated from West Point joining the USA Cavalry while also pursuing an athletic career, representing America in the modern pentathlon at the 1912 Stockholm Olympics.

Although he enjoyed a distinguished career during the Mexican Revolution and the First World War it was his exploits in the Second World War that made him a folk hero in his native country. He came to prominence during the North African and Sicily Campaigns and quickly became the man that the German high command feared most. As a consequence when plans were being drawn up for the D-Day landings in 1944 Patton was given command of a 'phantom army'. Through a series of double agents the German were led to believe that Patton was in Dover and that it was from there that the invasion would be launched thereby tying down the German 15th Army at Calais while in fact the attack was launched in Normandy.

Patton did enter that fray on 1 August leading the U.S. Third Army and began a drive south that saw them engaged in fighting for 281 consecutive days, including playing a major role in the Battle of the Bulge, capturing huge swathes of German occupied territory including 12000 cities and towns. In the process close on one and a half million German soldiers were captured or killed with a loss of life of only two thousand American personnel. Patton was not only a clever military strategist he was clearly a charismatic leader who inspired his men through a series of celebrated speeches which usually culminated with the words:

Then there's one thing you men will be able to say when this war is over and you get back home. Thirty years from now when you're sitting by your fireside with your grandson on your knee and he asks, 'What did you do in the great World War Two?' You won't have to cough and say, 'Well, your granddaddy shovelled shit in Louisiana.' No sir, you can look him straight in the eye and say 'Son, your granddaddy rode with the great Third Army and a son-of-a-goddamned-bitch named George Patton!'

Second World War General George S. Patton

As soon as the war in Europe was over Patton asked to be re-assigned to the continuing conflict in the Pacific but much to his disgust his request was refused and he was made Military Governor of Bavaria, a job he hated. His love of battle is clear from the statement he made on hearing that Japan had surrendered; while the rest of the Western world celebrated Patton commented *"Yet another war has come to an end and with it my usefulness to the world."*

In December 1945 Patton was invited to go on a pheasant hunting trip but the car in which he was travelling collided with an Army truck. As the car had been going at a slow speed those in the vehicle suffered very minor injuries with the sole exception of Patton who hit his head on a glass partition and in the process fractured his spine leaving him totally paralysed. Twelve days later he passed away in a local hospital and was buried at his request 'with his men' in the American cemetery in Luxembourg City. He was aged 60. It was an ignominious end for a war hero who had faced enemy fire in several continents and emerged relatively unscathed.

Patton was gone but certainly not forgotten and few military men have been depicted so often in films and on TV, and by such a diverse range of actors. These include the likes of Kirk Douglas in *Is Paris Burning?*, George Kennedy in *Brass Target* and most recently Kelsey Grammer in *An American Carol*. In case anyone has difficulty in imagining 'Frasier' playing 'Old Blood and Guts' it should be explained that it is a parody of the celebrated Dickens book with Patton appearing as one of the ghosts.

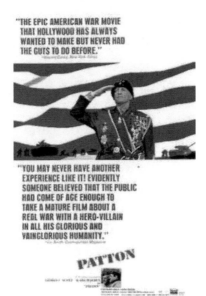

The most famous of all movies about the man, however, is undoubtedly the 1970 film titled *Patton* with George C. Scott in the title role. It won seven Academy Awards including Best Picture, Best Director for Franklin J. Schaffner and Best Actor for George C. Scott although he refused to accept the Oscar. The film was also a major box office hit further reinforcing the legacy of the remarkable George S. Patton.

But there is another equally interesting lineage from Hugh Mercer. His grandson, also called Hugh, was a military man serving as a Confederate officer but having survived the war he moved in later life to Baden Baden in Germany where he died. His family, however, remained in the American Deep South as it began to rebuild itself after the destruction suffered during the Civil War and his grandson, George Anderson Mercer, was a well known attorney and property developer in Savannah, Georgia. His second wife, who was previously his secretary, was a Croatian immigrant called Lillian and she bore him a son on 18 November 1909. The boy was named John but always called Johnny. Yes Johnny Mercer.

Mercer had a keen interest in music from a very early age and by the time he was six years old he was singing in a local choir. He was clearly influenced by his mother who loved to sing sentimental ballads and by his father who favoured old Scots songs no doubt handed down through the generations. Being brought up in Savannah the boy also heard a great deal of black music and was often to be found in record shops frequented by the African American community returning with discs by the likes of Ma Rainey, Bessie Smith and Louis Armstrong.

It was planned that Johnny would attend Princeton University until the vagaries of the financial situation in the 1920's meant that his father was unable to afford the fees. So instead the nineteen year old lad headed for New York City and settled in a rather rundown apartment in Greenwich Village with only a few sticks of furniture but fortunately a beat-up piano which allowed him to pursue his ambition to be a songwriter. He secured a day job with a brokerage firm and performed in the evenings; in addition to being a songwriter Mercer also possessed a good singing voice. But even after pooling their meagre income, Mercer and his roommate often existed on little more than oatmeal.

His first break came courtesy of a musical revue called *The Garrick Gaieties,* providing the lyrics for one of the songs in the score which was subsequently recorded. More importantly he met a chorus girl called Ginger Meehan who was being pursued by Bing Crosby, as were several of the other members of the chorus line, and two years later Ginger and Johnny were married and remained so until Mercer passed away forty five years later. Mercer and his wife had no family of their own but after ten childless years adopted a young girl they named Amanda but who was always called Mandy. She was the subject of the first big hit record by Mercer's close friend Barry Manilow.

With money tight in the years after they were wed his wife gave up the life of a chorus girl and worked as a seamstress while the couple moved in with her mother in Brooklyn to try and make ends meet. His break came when he got the opportunity to team up with established writer Hoagy Carmichael and one of their first collaborations 'Lazybones' became an instant hit and netted the writers $1250 each, a not inconsiderable sum in the early 1930's. However, his move into the big time came when he was offered the chance to go west, to Hollywood, and to write for the burgeoning movie industry.

After a couple of false starts he hit pay dirt when he wrote 'I'm An Old Cowhand from the Rio Grande' which Bing Crosby sang in the film *Rhythm on the Range* and Mercer followed it up the same year with another highly successful song 'Goody Goody'. From there the hit songs poured out in steady stream – 'Too Marvellous For Words', 'Hooray For Hollywood', 'You Must Have Been A Beautiful Baby' and 'Jeepers Creepers', the last named earning him an Oscar Nomination.

While in Hollywood, Mercer was able to rub shoulders with the great and the not-so-good of tinsel town and got involved in a much publicised affair with Judy Garland who, despite being only nineteen years old, was already engaged to composer and orchestra leader David Rose. In order to get Garland away from Mercer Rose quickly tied the knot with the charismatic singer and movie star. Mercer was obviously smitten by Garland as was clear from the lyrics of a number of the songs he subsequently wrote with 'I Remember You', a huge hit record for Australian Frank Ifield in 1962, dedicated to Judy.

Johnny Mercer

While largely concentrating on composing Mercer continued to sing and recorded a number of duets with Crosby while still able to turn out memorable songs such as 'Skylark', 'Come Rain or Come Shine', 'That All Black Magic' and 'On the Atchison, Topeka and the Santa

Fe', a huge hit for Judy Garland and another Oscar winner for John Mercer. He went on to win four such awards.

In 1942 he added yet another string to his bow when he founded Capitol Records but by the 1950's the emergence of rock and roll meant that there was less of a demand for the clever and witty lyrics for which Johnny had become famous. That said he did come up with some vintage songs such as 'Charade', 'Days of Wine and Rose' and 'The Shadow of Your Smile' as well as contributing to the score of the musical *Seven Brides for Seven Brothers*.

Mercer died on 25 June 1976 in Hollywood, aged 66, from an inoperable brain tumour and was buried in the Bonaventure Cemetery in Savannah where a memorial bench is adorned by a simple self portrait.

Self portrait on the memorial bench at Bonaventure Cemetery

During an extraordinary career Mercer is thought to have penned lyrics for some 1500 songs including many which are not only well remembered but are still performed regularly to this day.

But above them all is one song that is truly timeless, recorded by Frank Sinatra, Judy Garland and many others of that ilk and in more recent times by the likes of Sarah Brightman, Amy Winehouse and Melody Gardot. But the iconic version of the song will always be the original with Audrey Hepburn, in the movie *Breakfast at Tiffany's,* sitting on a window sill accompanying herself on guitar and singing of her 'huckleberry friend'. The song is of course 'Moon River' a wonderful piece of writing about a waterway many miles and several centuries from the sea off the Buchan shoreline where Johnny Mercer's Great Great Great Grandfather once paddled as a child.

Hugh Mercer Memorial at Laurel Hill Cemetery Philadelphia

James Scott Skinner

(1843-1927)

The Strathspey King

The elderly kilted gentleman marched on to the stage carrying his violin, ready to perform in a reel and jig contest for an expectant American audience. He quickly made it clear to all concerned, however, that he wasn't happy with the rules or with the accompanying pianist and strode off stage without playing a single note before returning home to Aberdeen. This wasn't a tantrum by some ill tempered youth but rather the actions of an octogenarian who had led a colourful if irascible life.

James Skinner, better known by the adopted name of Scott Skinner, was born in Arbeadie, a small village on the outskirts of Banchory, on 5 August 1843, the sixth and last child of William and Mary. His father was a gardener and dance teacher who suffered an accident with a shotgun as consequence of which he lost three fingers of his left hand and had to teach himself to play the fiddle with the damaged hand holding the bow instead of the instrument.

Eighteen months after James entered the world his father died and seven years later his mother, who hailed from Strathdon, remarried. James was sent to Aberdeen to live with his sister Annie where he attended Connell's School on Princes Street. He was taught to play the fiddle and the cello by his brother Alexander, who was ten years his senior, and by the age of eight James had become sufficiently proficient to be asked by fiddler Peter Milne to accompany him at local dances.

Unfortunately due to the absence of halls or other suitable venues in the area these events were normally held in barns and it was not unusual for James to have to walk up to ten miles carrying his instrument to play, and then the same distance back home later. For this he was paid the princely sum of five shillings, the equivalent of 25 pence in today's currency, per month. Despite receiving such a pittance he became fond of Milne, viewing him as a surrogate father and he often fetched 'medicine' as his mentor like to call the opium he was addicted to.

Clearly James grew up fast, auditioning at the suggestion of his brother Sandy for a children's orchestra known as *Dr. Mark's Little Men* and in 1855 he signed up for a six year apprenticeship based in Manchester; he was only eleven years old when he headed south. The average day for the boys comprised of a morning of general education and play, followed by a similar afternoon but with a concert thrown in. Most evenings were given over to performing for the public with the group touring the length and breadth of Britain. While James, or the 'kilted boy' as he became known, benefitted from the musical tuition and the chance to play, life was not always happy down in Manchester and on one occasion he was sent home following a fist fight with one of his fellow musicians.

Latterly during his spell in Manchester he became friendly with French violinist Charles Rougier from the famed Halle Orchestra who, on realising that the boys in the 'Little Men' group were purely taught to play by ear, set about teaching Skinner to read music and to play pieces by Beethoven and other classical composers. In later years Skinner admitted that without Rougier's teaching he would never have been able to compose. It was at that stage that James decided to quit the apprenticeship with the Little Men several months before it was officially due to be completed heading straight into yet another episode of what eventually proved to be a highly colourful life.

In the 1830's in America a form of entertainment called *The Minstrel Show* was invented and through the next one hundred and fifty years it became hugely popular. The idea seems to have been to show the white population of the Northern part of the States and most of the Western world, who had no knowledge of Negroes or their way life, how they lived and behaved. Due to an absence of coloured entertainers their places were largely taken by white people with their faces blackened and with large white lips painted on.

In the shows the coloured people were generally depicted as happy but dim-witted as they clowned around and sang what was rather unsubtly known as 'coon' songs mixed with a sprinkling of spirituals and Stephen Foster favourites like 'Camptown Races' and 'Suwannee River'. The shows, which became hugely popular and resulted in Minstrel Show troupes being formed around the world, normally boasted the same standard stereotypes such as the big fat 'Mammy' and the runaway slave.

Black face minstrels

Modern day audiences would clearly be horrified by the whole concept and yet as recently as 1978 a show derived from this format was peak Saturday night entertainment on BBC television. George Mitchell's *Black and White Minstrel Show* premiered on TV in 1958 and within a matter of four years was also a hugely successful stage show, running at London's Victoria Palace Theatre continuously for ten years. In addition it toured the country, being particularly popular in summer months at seaside resorts, and even ventured as far as Australia and New Zealand.

A by-product of this TV success was sound recordings and in the seventies there probably weren't many houses in the UK that didn't 'boast' a *Black and White Minstrels* L.P. Indeed their first three albums all topped the UK charts often retaining the number one spot for weeks or months at a time. But slowly resentment at the depicting of coloured people in this manner began to gain momentum and by 1978 the show was shelved and is now an embarrassment to the Beeb not that the BBC is easily embarrassed.

In 1861 Skinner was soon blacking up in this manner as he went on tour as part of the New Orleans Theatre Company but it was a relatively short lived engagement and he opted to come back to Aberdeen. On returning north he caught up with Peter Milne who recommended that James add another string to his fiddle bow and to learn dancing and James enrolled with Willie Scott, a man who called himself a 'Professor of Dance'. James Skinner was so impressed by his new teacher that he decided to adopt the man's surname as an alternate Christian name and so J. Scott Skinner emerged and remained the rest of his days. Under his dance teacher's guidance Skinner soon became highly proficient and indeed within a year had won a Highland dance competition in Ireland and a Strathspey and Reel contest in Inverness. Encouraged by his success he established a professional dance school in the remote Aberdeenshire village of Strathdon; the village was originally called Invernochty and the area enjoyed prominence in more recent times when Billy Connolly bought Candacraig House to which he would invite his Hollywood pals to enjoy the annual Lonach Gathering. Back in the 1860's,

Skinner was also rubbing shoulders with the rich and famous as he began giving dance lessons at Balmoral Castle.

Two years after Queen Victoria married Prince Albert the couple began their long term love affair with Scotland, frequently staying in the likes of Edinburgh and in Blair Castle. Following a holiday in Loch Laggan where it rained incessantly the Queen's physician suggested that they look to Deeside and its 'drier climate' (obviously the man had a sense of humour) and Prince Albert came across Balmoral Castle, sited on the banks of the River Dee between Ballater and Braemar, negotiating with Lord Aberdeen to take over the lease.

The Second Balmoral Castle

The couple enjoyed their first holiday there in 1848 in a building which pre-dated the current monolith. Although the original was less grand it was still worthy of the title of 'Castle' and yet was described by Victoria as 'pretty but small'; clearly the lassie never bade in twa rooms with a place on the stair. While they liked the area, the arrival of additional Royal mouths to feed with metronomic regularity, the Queen eventually giving birth to nine children, coupled with the need for shed loads of servants resulted in the requirement for constant extensions and improvements until in 1852 a decision was made to build a new Balmoral Castle.

A site was chosen 100 yards from the exiting property and after four years of construction the grand affair that stands to this day was completed at which stage the original Castle was summarily demolished. Victoria and Albert both loved life in the new property and were known to spend up to four months there in the summer and autumn. Their daily routine would involve the Queen going on long walks, often up to four hours at a time, around the 50000 acre estate while Albert would go off and slaughter the local wildlife. Evenings were often given over to dances and musical entertainments and that is when Skinner found himself immersed in the Balmoral lifestyle thanks in no small measure to a certain Mr. Brown.

In 1861, after twenty one years of marriage, Prince Albert died aged just 42. The Queen was devastated and spent a long time in mourning during which she regularly visited Balmoral and became friendly with a man called John Brown.

Born at Crathie, near the Castle, in 1826 and from a humble background, Brown became ghillie for the Royal household and was there to offer help and support to the grieving widow. Over the next twenty years they became very close although there is no evidence to support the rumours that their relationship was other than platonic. It was yet another blow to Queen Victoria when Brown took ill and died just 56 years old and she wrote:

'He had no thought but for me, my welfare, my comfort, my safety, my happiness. Courageous, unselfish, totally disinterested, discreet to the highest degree, speaking the truth fearlessly and telling me what he thought and considered to be "just and right," without flattery and without saying what would be pleasing if he did not think it right. . . . The comfort of my daily life is gone—the void is terrible—the loss is irreparable'.

The Queen had a life size statue of John Brown, whose relationship with Victoria was depicted in the Billy Connolly/ Judy Dench film *Mrs. Brown,* erected in the grounds of Balmoral but after she died her son Edward VII, who was clearly jealous of their relationship, had it moved to a less conspicuous site and also had other memorials to the man destroyed.

Skinner would later recall his friendship with Brown and in particular an evening when he was performing in the Castle before Queen Victoria and her guest the Duchess of Atholl. Brown pushed Skinner close to where the two women sat saying 'Noo Skinner, ye're in the richt quarter noo. Shak' yer fit man, shak' yer fit.' Clearly he must have shaken his foot rather well as he was engaged as dance instructor and given the task of teaching dance to tenants of Balmoral Estate together with their children, providing him with 125 new pupils.

Statue to John Brown at Balmoral Castle

In 1871 Skinner married Jean Stewart who came from the village of Aberlour and that same year a daughter named Jeannie was born while a son called Manson arrived ten years later. By that time the Skinner family had moved to Elgin, choosing the Moray town because of its rail links. Thanks to the expansion of railway along the East of Scotland Skinner was able to establish dancing schools as far north as Wick in Caithness as well as Nairn, Inverness, Tain and other points in between.

Skinner was never famed for his tolerance as many of his pupils who, despite their parents paying substantial sums for the lessons, would attest, finding themselves the recipient of a rap on the head from a fiddle bow if they made a mistake with their dance steps. He was, however, fortunate enough to enjoy the patronage of many of the wealthy families living in that North East corner of Scotland and when not arriving by train he would appear in a smart carriage pulled by an elegant pony. At that time he was earning £750 per annum, a very respectable income by 19th Century standards.

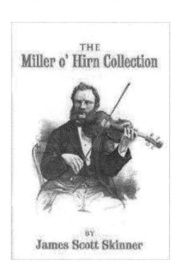

As early as 1860 when just seventeen years old Skinner had began composing his own tunes, the first being titled 'Highland Polka'. Five years later 'The Ettrick Vale Quadrilles' appeared in print followed in 1881 during his heyday by his first collection under the name of 'The Miller o' Hirn Collection'.

Skinner in his heyday

In 1884 he brought out a number of works but it was the somewhat ambitious 'The Elgin Collection' that had a major effect on his life as high productions costs and lower than expected sales left him bankrupt and more than £150 in debt. He later described the event as *'in a single day I was roofless, wifeless and penniless'.*

The loss of a spouse came about as a direct result of his financial misfortunate, Jean suffering nervous exhaustion as a consequence of the trauma and being admitted to Elgin Asylum. She never recovered and aged 58 died in the asylum on 5 January 1899. A mere six months later Skinner married Gertrude Mary Park, whom he had met while staying in Union Grove in Aberdeen, and the couple moved to Monikie in Angus. It was not to be a happy marriage. Skinner would not have been an easy man to live with, clearly unburdened by modesty; he frequently referred to himself as a 'genius' and on one occasion declared that 'with the exception of myself there was no Scottish violinist of any eminence at this time'.

Whatever the reason his wife left him, or 'resigned from the marriage' as she precisely put it, and moved to Rhodesia in 1909 while around the same time his son Manson emigrated to Australia. His daughter Jeannie did, however, stick by her father and helped organise his dance classes with the assistance of his late brother Sandy's widow, Madame de Lenglee.

In the difficult years after his bankruptcy when he couldn't even afford to publish sheet music of his own compositions he decided to try his luck in America but the tour was a disaster although it did convince Skinner that he should forget about dancing and concentrate on his fiddle playing. His failure in the States must have been a blow to him especially when a close friend and fellow Scot had conquered the USA to such an extent that by 1911 he was the highest paid entertainer in the world. He was, of course, Harry Lauder.

Lauder was born on 4 August 1870 in Portobello near Edinburgh, the eldest of seven children, and christened Henry Lauder. His was the ultimate rags-to-riches story; at age ten he was working in a coal mine for ten shillings (50p) a week and thirty years later at the height of his fame he was regularly earning a thousand pound in a single night. He spent a decade working in the mines, witnessing the death of fellow miners in the unhealthy and dangerous pits, but had at least the good fortunate to make the acquaintance of Ann Vallance, the daughter of colliery manager in Hamilton, who he married in 1891.

The couple had one child, a boy named John, who was made a Captain in Argyll and Sutherland Regiment during the First World

War but was killed in action 1916. His death prompted Lauder to write a song which, for once, wasn't flippant or comic, and '*Keep Right on to the End of the Road*' became a War anthem.

While still working as a miner he was also regularly appearing at music halls in the Hamilton and Larkhall areas as a singer and comedian and encouraged by the favourable reaction he enjoyed from audiences he turned professional in 1894. Life was, however, tough for the couple until Lauder decided to venture to London where he was an almost instant success albeit through sheer hard work; on occasions he would appear in six different music halls in a single night, travelling between them by pony and trap. He was particularly well received in the like of the Charing Cross Music Hall and the London Pavilion but when the opportunity arose to appear in the 1905 Pantomime at the Theatre Royal in Glasgow he jumped at the chance to return to Scotland. The show proved a great success with Lauder debuting what became his signature tune, '*I Love a Lassie*'.

By 1907 he was touring America commanding fees of $1000 a night and by 1912 he was top of the bill at the first ever Royal Command Performance before King George V. He also enjoyed great success in Australia and was there when the First World War broke out and during the next four years he worked to raise money for a fund established to help injured servicemen. Recognition of his charitable efforts resulted in a knighthood in 1919.

While continuing to tour during his later years, dying in 1950 aged 79, he also appeared in three movies together with a short film alongside Charlie Chaplin, made a number of sound recordings and wrote several books. His funeral in Hamilton was widely reported by the likes of Pathe News and wreaths were sent by many dignitaries including the Queen Mother and Winston Churchill. And yet all these years later he remains a controversial figure.

Winston Churchill described him as 'Scotland's greatest ever ambassador' a boast that would be contested by many. But Churchill wasn't the only person who was a fan of Lauder. Fellow singer and comedian Jimmy Logan was inspired by his hero to pursue a stage career and in the seventies wrote and starred in a one man show titled 'Lauder' which, thanks to producer Cameron Mackintosh, toured widely.

But if Churchill and Logan were in the pro-Lauder camp on the other side there was a queue of people who were, and still are, very anti. The problem is that Lauder's stage persona was based on a pastiche of Scotland and in particular Scots, appearing in an exaggerated Highland dress topped off with a Tam O'Shanter bonnet and a crooked walking stick. He was a comic figure that sang trite songs like *Roamin' in the Gloamin* and *Stop Yer Ticklin' Jock* in best *Brigadoon* style and personified the Scottish race as ultra parsimonious.

Jimmy Logan's stage tribute to Lauder

Scottish poet Hugh MacDiarmid was a particularly vociferous critic of the man describing 'Lauderism' as having made *'thousands of*

Scotsmen so disgusted that they have gone to the opposite extreme and become, or tried to become, as English as possible'. Just as unhappy with Lauder was comedian Stanley Baxter who described Lauder as *'phoney baloney'* and as a man *'who sang of his granny's heilan hame and the mountains and glens and yet never lived north of Rutherglen'.*

Harry Lauder dressed as a 'typical' Scottish man

What no one can argue with is the success that Lauder enjoyed in sojourns across the Atlantic; sadly the same could not be said of Scott Skinner whose tour of the States in 1893 was a catastrophe. He went to the States with piper and champion Highland dancer Willie MacLennan but his fellow performer took ill and died of meningitis. The tour subsequently collapsed and Skinner was forced to rely on the financial assistance of a number of wealthy ex-pat Scots to pay for his passage home. That left him even poorer than before a situation which was not appreciated by his second wife, no doubt contributing to her decision to leave her husband and move to Africa. After her departure Skinner roamed around the country giving concerts and living wherever he could, often ending up staying in houses of friends.

By 1899 he had begun to record many of his compositions, one of the first Scottish artists to do so, and continued to record for most of his remaining days. He also penned an autobiography called '*My Life and Adventures*' and despite the fact that he was in his eightieth year he bought the first house he ever owned. It was at 25 Victoria Street, Aberdeen and he set up home there with housekeeper Mrs Lily Richards.

Scott Skinner's autobiography

In 1911 at the suggestion of Harry Lauder he formed *The Caledonian Four* who were asked to perform at the opening of the Palladium Theatre in London. But that was an all too brief moment of late stardom although in the 1920's despite his advancing years he was still performing and often undertaking UK tours although these events weren't always financial successes. Indeed in 1924 he returned from a tour of England that included an appearance in the Royal Albert Hall declaring that he had lost £200 on the tour but that '*there were greater losses at Culloden*'.

Skinner died at his home in Aberdeen on 17 March 1927 and was buried in Allenvale Cemetery. He left behind a remarkable treasure chest of fiddle tunes, some 600 in number, including famous works like *The Music o' Spey, Cradle Song* and *Hector the Hero*, the last named a lament to honour his friend Major-General Hector MacDonald who committed suicide after being accused of being a homosexual.

Many of these tunes are still performed to this day by renowned musicians, the most notable being Paul Anderson who discovered a fiddle under a bed in his grandparents' farm house in Tarland and was instantly hooked. He still plays that same instrument to this day.

Paul followed the path of Skinner by composing Scottish fiddle music and to date has written over 300 tunes and recorded eight solo albums. He has also contributed music to films, TV programmes and stage productions and his association with his predecessor goes even further as Paul appeared on stage in the play *The Strathspey King* about Skinner's life. Paul Anderson's talent was recognised by the Royal family, being asked to perform at Prince Charles's 60th Birthday Party in Fyvie Castle, and by the Scottish Government who commissioned him to appear in Edinburgh Castle at a similar celebration to mark the 80th Birthday of Sir Sean Connery.

Skinner's native Banchory has remembered their famous son by creating the Scott Skinner Square, a quiet spot to sit and escape the hustle and bustle of the nearby High Street while an impressive memorial, partly financed by public donations, was erected at

Allenvale Cemetery four years after his death. It includes a bronze bust together with a depiction of a violin and part of the music from one Skinner's most famous compositions, *The Bonnie Lass o' Bon Accord*. The depth of their friendship and the esteem in which he held Skinner was displayed by the fact that Sir Harry Lauder ventured north of Rutherglen to perform the unveiling.

Memorial at Allenvale Cemetery

Thomas Blake Glover (1838-1911)

'

From the North East to the Far East

In the garden of a bungalow perched on a hill overlooking the harbour of the Japanese city of Nagasaki stands a beautifully crafted statue of a woman dressed in traditional costume with a small boy by her side. The statue is of Tamaki Miura, a Japanese opera singer who garnered fame as Cio-Cio San, the tragic heroine of the opera *Madame Butterfly*.

A statue in a garden so distant from the North East of Scotland would appear to be irrelevant to this book if it wasn't for the fact that the villa in question is one of the most visited tourist attractions in Japan simply because it was once the home of the man born in another, and rather different, coastal town six thousand miles away.

On 13 December 1911 in an elegant and impressive house in the Azabu district of Tokyo a petit servant entered his master's bedroom, placed a tray with a bowl of soup on a small table, bowed and left. When the servant returned to remove the tray a few minutes later he discovered that the elderly gentleman was slumped across the table and efforts to revive him failed. The gentleman who peacefully passed away three days later on 16 December was Thomas Blake Glover.

Like so many other famous people over the years, Glover came from the 'Broch', born in 15 Commerce Street, Fraserburgh on 6 June 1838. The adjacent building round the corner on Broad Street, which now houses the Glover & Co chip shop, boasts a blue plaque commemorating the event. Thomas was the fifth son born to Thomas Berry Glover, who was in charge of the local Coastguard Station, and his wife Mary, although by the time he appeared only three survived, Henry having died as an infant. The position that his father occupied was clearly both prestigious and financially lucrative as the couple were able to send the three eldest boys to Aberdeen Grammar School as boarders while Thomas stayed behind and enjoyed an education at the local school.

Madame Butterfly statue in the garden of Glover House in Nagasaki

When his father was promoted to look after the Coastguard Station in Aberdeen the Glover clan moved to a property in Bridge of Don just over the River Don from Old Aberdeen and the younger children, Tom included, enrolled at the Gymnasium School in the Chanonry about a mile away. Despite its name it was not an establishment purely for the teaching of physical education but pursued a more comprehensive curriculum along the lines of Gymnasia centres in Germany providing a wide range of options both classical and practical. The building also referred to on occasions as the Chanonry School closed in 1887 and now forms part of the Cruickshank Botanical Garden belonging to the University of Aberdeen.

After three years and having reached the age of sixteen Tom Glover secured work as a clerk with the internal trading company of Jardine Matheson & Co. at their offices in Marischal Street Aberdeen; the company subsequently became a multinational conglomerate with their worldwide headquarters now established in Hong Kong. The young Glover must have impressed his bosses as within a couple of years and while still in his teens, he was despatched to the company's office in Shanghai. Tom was delighted with the opportunity to see the world and to hopefully make his fortune.

In 1857 when Tom arrived in Shanghai, which literally means 'on the sea', the city was already a large bustling metropolis and the major commercial centre in China. It must have proved quite a culture shock and a rude awakening, in more ways than one, for the young lad from the tranquil North East of Scotland especially Shanghai's notorious district which had garnered the unenviable title of 'Blood Alley' where visiting seamen gathered for recreation and where the company of girls as young as twelve could be bought for a few pence.

Shanghai did, however, provide Glover with an education in the ways of foreign trade and being a quick learner within two years his employers offered him the chance to move to Japan.

From the early part of the 17th century, as a consequence of edicts introduced by the ruling Shogun, Japan was more or less a closed country with foreigners prevented from visiting or even trading with it and the vast majority of Japanese people banned from leaving. However by 1853 the rules were slowly being relaxed, in particular through the southerly port of Nagasaki to which Thomas Glover was dispatched.

It would be nice to report that Nagasaki is best known for the novelty song of that title penned by the American writing duo of Harry Warren and Mort Dixon which reports that in Nagasaki *'the men chew tobaccy and the women wicky-wacky woo'*. Sadly that is not the case and the city will always be remembered for the events of 9 August 1945.

In an effort to force the Japanese Government to surrender and consequently bring the six year world war to an end the U.S. decided to drop two Atomic bombs and the cities of Hiroshima and Kokura were chosen as the targets. The former was bombed on 6 August and the second mission began three days later. A faulty reserve fuel tank pump on *Bookscar,* the plane carrying the deadly weapon, delayed the flight and by the time on 9 August that it arrived over Kokura cloud and smoke from earlier air raids reduced visibility to such an extent that the target could not be located.

After 50 fruitless minutes of flying in the face of heavy enemy bombardment and with fuel running out, a decision was made to leave Kokura and head towards Nagasaki. It was also decided that if cloud persisted over Nagasaki making it impossible to accurately drop the bomb that the mission was to be aborted and the bomb would be jettisoned in the ocean.

At 11.02 on that fateful day the cloud over Nagasaki suddenly cleared and the Atomic bomb was dropped. It is estimated that close on 74000 citizens died in Nagasaki and about 140000 perished in Hiroshima while countless others in both cities suffered long term health problems as a consequence of radiation poisoning.

On arriving in Nagasaki Glover joined up with a fellow Scot Kenneth Ross MacKenzie who had earlier established an office of Jardine Matheson dealing in various commodities although initial tea was the main product that they bought and exported. That may have seemed a rather mundane substance to build a business on bearing in mind how commonplace and cheap it is today but back in the nineteenth century the situation was very different. Indeed in that era it was not oil but tea that could be described as black gold.

Tea drinking became fashionable in the west during the 17th century but a combination of the high cost of importing it from the Far East and prohibitive taxes meant inevitably that smugglers would get involved and long before opium became the chosen product of the criminal elements tea was being smuggled into the UK in enormous quantities. Always anxious to increase their profit margins smugglers began mixing tea leaves with leaves from other plants and when they encountered complaints about the colour of their product which wasn't dark enough compared with the real thing, they added copper carbonate, unconcerned that it was a poisonous substance, and even sheep dung.

High taxes weren't the only problem facing men like Glover who were engaged in the legal tea trade. Tea leaves had to be dried before they embarked on the lengthy sea voyages to the West which greatly added to the cost. Ever a step ahead of most of his contemporaries, Glover established his own drying plant in Nagasaki and became heavily involved with the commodity, employing over 1000 tea pickers at one time. And yet throughout his life he experienced difficulty in making the business profitable.

In addition to tea Glover became involved in the exportation of seaweed and silk, mainly to Chinese coastal cities while, to ensure that the company vessels didn't return empty, he imported medicines, cotton and sugar to Japan. When MacKenzie decided to return to China, Glover took over the role of Jardine Matheson's agent in Nagasaki before breaking away from his employer and establishing his own company, Glover & Co.

Glover House in Nagasaki

Settled in Nagasaki Glover designed and built a house on the hill overlooking the harbour; the house was known as 'Ipponmatsu' which translates as 'Lone Pine' so called because a solitary pine tree was incorporated into the design. Within a matter of years Glover & Co. prospered and before long there were three Glovers working in Japan under that name as two of Thomas's brothers, Jim and Alexander, travelled there to work with him while William and Charles subsequently became involved with the business, the later from afar. And as soon as the youngest of the six sons, Alfred, had completed his schooling he also headed for the land of the rising sun.

Mary Glover had given birth to seven boys, six of whom survived to adulthood, and must have been delighted in 1842 when at last a daughter, Martha Anne, came along. Aged eighteen the girl married a local ship broker called James George and the couple had three children, one of whom died as an infant, although sadly she was widowed at an early age. Thomas, who was very fond of his sister, regularly invited her to move to Japan but Martha behaved as a dutiful daughter by remaining in Scotland to look after her aging parents. Shortly after both of them had passed away Martha's life was shattered when her daughter Annie died aged just twenty two and she made the decision to go to Japan, staying initially with Thomas who had moved to Tokyo, and latterly with her brother Alfred in Nagasaki where she died in 1903 and was buried in Sakamota International Cemetery.

Glover Family Group (left to right Martha, Tomisaburo, Hana, Thomas with grandchild and Waka)

Although Japan had been opened to Westerners many locals were initially unhappy with the situation and anti-foreign fanatics expressed their feelings with direct action. In the month that Glover arrived in Nagasaki two Russian sailors were murdered while a British national was slain outside the office of Jardine Matheson in Yokohama. But as far as violence was concerned far worse lay ahead and Glover found himself, at his own volition, at the centre of it.

For centuries Japan had been ruled by the iron fist of the Shogun but slowly during the 19th century the supreme leader's control began to slacken as unrest grew around the country especially in the south west where a rebellion was led by members of the Satsuma clan. Glover realised that if the rebels, who were deeply unhappy with the ruling Imperial Government, were to have any chance of succeeding then they would have to be armed and Glover saw a unique opportunity. He began by importing guns but soon began to think bigger. He was able to negotiate the sale of a second hand steamer the *S.S. Sarah* to the clan and subsequently, with the assistance of his brother Charles who was a well established shipping agent in Aberdeen, organised the building of a new vessel at the William Duthie Jr. shipyard in the Scottish city. The vessel named the *Satsuma* sailed to Japan under the command of yet another Glover sibling, William.

Although Glover had sympathy for the rebels he was never one to turn his back on a way of making money and so he also helped arm the government forces. Fortunately for him the rebels prevailed, eventually leading to the role of the Shogun being abolished and in the process Glover achieved hero status and the title of the 'Scottish Samurai'.

When relative peace was restored in the country Glover continued to prosper commercially but his personal life developed in somewhat turbulent ways. I think it is fair to assume that any lady of a feminist persuasion would be truly horrified by the level of male chauvinism that greeted Glover in Japan. Quite simply a local girl could be invited to become a Westerner's wife but then pushed aside without a buy-your-leave as soon as the 'gentleman' tired of the arrangement or when his wandering eye alighted on someone new and more to his fancy. Glover was happy to go along with this arrangement and within a relatively short time of his arrival had entered into such a 'marriage ceremony' with a girl called Sono Hiranga.

The couple had a son together who they named Umekichi but tragically the boy died when he was four months old. It was a relatively short lived affair and before long the couple 'divorced'. It appears to have been an amicable parting, however, as years later Glover paid for his ex-wife to travel abroad to study. Free from the ties that bind the lad from Aberdeen sowed his wild oats for sometime before eventually settling down with another Nagasaki woman by the name of Yamamura Tsuru and they lived happily as husband and wife for 32 years until she sadly died in 1899.

Glover's wife Tsura

Together they had a daughter whom they named Hana but unfortunately Glover's wife was unable to have any further children.

Before he had married, Glover had an affair with a local geisha girl by the name of Maki Kaga who bore him a son she called Shinzaburo and although Glover made no effort to marry the girl he didn't desert either the mother or son and regularly contributed financial to the boy's upbringing.

By the time the lad was five years old Glover was forced to accept that his wife couldn't bear him the son he desperately wanted to carry on the family name and business. For that reason he went to see Maki Kaga and advised her that he would be taking the boy from her and raising him in his home as his son. Not surprisingly the girl was far from pleased by such a suggestion and implored Glover not to take the boy but her pleas fell on deaf ears. How exactly she reacted to this decision remains a matter of some speculation although it has been suggested by some biographers that she dressed the boy in his finest clothes, covered his eyes with a blind fold and then cut her own throat although she was discovered in time and survived. Despite these harrowing events Glover was unrepentant and took the boy away, renaming him Tomisaburo.

Now opera buffs may feel that they have seen this scene played out on stage and in many ways they have courtesy of one the world's greatest composers Giacomo Puccini in arguably his finest work, *Madame Butterfly*. The composer was born in Lucca in Tuscany on the 22nd of December 1858 and named Giacomo Antonio Domenico Michele Secondo Maria Puccini. He was one of family of eight and by the time the last one had arrived his parents must surely have been running out of names.

The Puccini family was steeped in music and it is not surprising that Giacomo followed along that path, studying initially in Lucca before going to the Milan conservatory. By the time he was 21 he had written a Mass and followed that with three operas which were well received although on a modest scale before adapting a book titled *La Vie de Boheme* at which point his career took off.

The four act work telling the story of four struggling artists and writers and the tragic Mimi living in a cold Parisian garret was an instant hit and *La Boheme* remains one of the most loved and most performed operas to this day. It also inspired Broadway writer Jonathan Larson to adapt the story and set it in modern day New York during the AIDS epidemic, the resultant work *Rent* becoming a huge success worldwide.

Puccini followed *La Boheme* with *Tosca* and it was while he was in London in 1900 attending a production of that opera that he was taken to Covent Garden to see a one act play titled *Madame Butterfly: A Tragedy of Japan* by renowned playwright David Belasco. Despite having difficulty in understanding some of the play which was performed in English Puccini was so enthralled by the piece that he asked to meet the playwright after the curtain fell and begged to be allowed to adapt it for his next opera. Not surprisingly in the light of Puccini's worldwide fame Belasco readily agreed.

Puccini wrote the opera in his impressive home, now a fascinating museum, on the shores of the beautiful lake at Torre del Lago in Tuscany and by the start of 1904 he was ready to reveal to the public what he believed was his masterwork choosing to do it at THE opera house, La Scala in Milan. Sadly the event didn't turn out as he had hoped as the opera was subject to abuse from a claque believed to have been hired by rival composers jealous of Puccini's success who greeted the opera with boos and catcalls. To avoid his beloved work suffering further ill-treatment he withdrew it after the one performance before returning to Torre del Lago, chastened and disillusioned, but still with belief in the opera's merits, to work on re-writes.

When *Madame Butterfly* reappeared several months later the second act had been split in two by the beautiful *Humming Chorus* and he chose a more modest venue, the Theater Grande in Brescia, for the second 'premiere'. It was an instant success and was being performed as far afield as New York and Sydney within a matter of a few years.

The composer died in Brussels on 19 November 1924 from complications arising from treatment he was undergoing for throat cancer; the man was a chain smoker of cigarettes and cigars throughout his adult life. At the time of his death he was close to completing *Turandot,* having already written *Nessun Dorma,* arguably opera's greatest aria, and the opera was completed by Franco Alfano. However, on its opening night at La Scala in Milan composer Toscanini laid down his baton and left the stage at the point in the libretto where Puccini had stopped writing.

Although the two men clearly never met, coming from very different backgrounds and living in different continents, Glover and Puccini had a great deal in common. Both were from a family of eight, had a love of good wines and smoking and hunting and both were serial womanisers. In a way that mirrored Glover's involvement with geisha girl Maki Kaga, Puccini became embroiled with a servant girl, in his case with tragic results.

Insanely jealous of her husband's affairs Elvira Puccini spread word that he was romantically involved with Doria Manfredi, a domestic servant she had hired, and despite the fact that the story had no substance the young girl took rat poison and after several days of agony she died. Elvira was taken to court, found guilty of slander and sentenced to five months in prison. It was only after Puccini persuaded the girl's family to drop the charges in exchange for 12000 lire that Elvira avoided incarceration. Puccini's action may have been prompted by a sense of guilt as he had been engaged in an affair with Giulia Manfredi, the poor servant girl's cousin. Puccini's wife simply accused the wrong person.

The debate about whether the fictional Lt. Pinkerton was inspired by Thomas Blake Glover rumbles on. Clearly the similarities between the central story of the opera and the incident in Glover's life of Maki

Giacomo and Elvira Puccini

Kaga and Tomisaburo are striking but there is far more to it than that. At the time when Glover reclaimed his son the relatively small number of Westerners who lived in Nagasaki had formed a close knit community, one that would have clearly known of everything that went on amongst their contemporaries. That group included a lady by the name of Jennie Correll, an American who lived in Nagasaki with her husband, a Methodist minister.

When Jennie returned to Philadelphia she told her brother about life and events in Japan. Her brother was John Luther Long who then wrote a short story titled *Madame Butterfly* which subsequently became a Belasco play and then the Puccini opera. Long was quoted as saying that the inspiration for his novel was a combination of the stories his sister told him about her time in Nagasaki and a book called *Madame Chrysantheme.* Several historians appear convinced that Glover was in fact the inspiration for Lt. Pinkerton which, of course, would then make him Chris Scott in *Miss Saigon,* as the Boublil and Schonberg musical is very much a modern re-make of the Puccini opera.

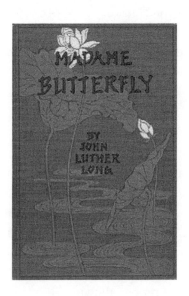

After the Japanese civil war Glover & Co. began diversifying and expanded their links with the Aberdeen ship yards commissioning vessels for trade rather than war. Glover clearly saw the potential in ship building and built the first dry dock in Japan so that the country would no longer be reliant on importing vessels from thousands of miles away. He also helped establish a coal mine, the first in Japan to be worked by British steam technology, which was built on Takashima Island situated nearly ten miles offshore from Nagasaki. It proved successful, eventually coming under the umbrella of the Mitsubishi Corporation.

One of the more interesting enterprises that Glover became involved with was the establishment of a brewery and not just any brewery but one that produced Kirin beer. The Dutch were the first to introduce the Japanese to beer and the locals quickly acquired a taste for it. An American by the name of William Copeland set up small company, the Spring Barley Brewery, in Yokohama until ill health forced him to close it down. Glover never did anything by halves and clearly saw an opportunity for a major operation, purchasing the defunct brewery and creating a new and large scale operation named the Japan Brewery Company which produced Kirin beer. It was an instant success and to this day, close on 150 years after it was first brewed, Kirin remains Japan's favourite beer while the brew is also available and enjoyed worldwide.

The extent of Glover's fortune can perhaps best be highlighted by a vanity project he embarked on; nowadays it would probably be the purchase of a Ferrari or a Lamborghini but Glover went one better with the acquisition of a steam engine. Not a toy one but the real thing which he had shipped from Britain to Japan despite the fact that it weighed in at just under 42 tons. Would love to have seen Amazon Prime offering free delivery on that. The engine called the *Iron Duke* was built for the Great Western Railway and entered service in 1847 before eventually being retired allowing Glover to step in.

The Iron Duke

Only problem was that there wasn't a length of track within a 100 miles of Nagasaki but undeterred Glover went and laid a short section of rails along the shoreline just below his house and had the engine run back and forth along it whenever the mood took him, on occasions taking the controls himself.

But his life was not one of unmitigated success and possibly due to a combination of too many fingers in too many pies and fearless risk taking he ended up in 1870 with debts of $500,000 and assets of only $200,000. The inevitable result was bankruptcy. Fortunately you can't keep a good man down and like a phoenix Glover rose from the ashes and quickly earned an even greater fortune the second time around and one that he succeeded on hanging on to until the end of his life. Although he spent much of his early years in Nagasaki, assisted by his siblings who followed their brother to Japan, he did return home to Aberdeen on occasions, combining the opportunity of seeing his mother and father with meetings with local ship builders and other business partners.

In 1876 Glover and family moved from Nagasaki to Tokyo to live in a palatial home in Azabu near Shiba Park from where he travelled in a grand horse and cart to his office. He left his youngest brother Alfred in charge of the Nagasaki office and although Alfred lacked his brother's entrepreneurial skills he soon became a well known and popular figure in the city especially amongst the English speaking fraternity.

Glover's home at Azabu, Tokyo

Alfred discovered that there were 13 other Scots living in Nagasaki, many of them from Aberdeen, and founded a St. Andrew's Society. Every year on 30 November he would organise a dinner and, as a pleasant change from Japanese fare with its dependence on rice and noodles would serve up roast beef, cheeses and even haggis which he managed to import.

At the same time and although semi retired, Thomas continued to work in Tokyo in the role of an advisor to an emerging company. One by the name of Mitsubishi.

Glover with Iwasaki Yatora (far left)

The company was founded in 1867 by Iwasaki Yatora and the name Mitsubishi can roughly be translated as three diamonds giving rise to the famous logo. It initially concentrated on ship building but soon began diversifying into other fields such as coal mining, through the acquisition of Glover's Takashima Mine, paper, steel, glass, electrical equipment, oil, and real estate. One of the more unsavoury chapters of the Mitsubishi story arose during the Second World War when the company began manufacturing fighter planes for the Imperial Japanese Navy using prisoners of war and Chinese citizens as forced labour.

After the war legal action was taken against the Japanese government but it wasn't until 2015 that an official apology about this practice was made to both China and America.

Post-war the company continued to flourish and currently there are some 40 companies under the Mitsubishi banner including the successful car maker and the camera manufacturer Nikon. Glover's contribution to the growth and success of Mitsubishi cannot be underrated and he was clearly greatly valued by its owners as in the role of 'advisor' he is said to have earned more than the chairman.

Glover was also valued significantly by the Japanese government and was recognised by them in 1908 when Emperor Meiji personally presented him with the Order of the Rising Sun Second Class, the highest honour that Japan can bestow on anyone not born in the country, and many subsequent photographs show him proudly wearing the medal.

Glover survived his wife by many years until he eventually passed away peacefully in 1911 as consequence of the kidney disease that had troubled him for some time.

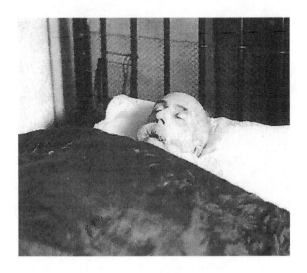

Glover on his death bed

He was survived by his daughter Hana, who had married a British business man Walter Gordon Bennett, and son Tomisaburo, who married Waka, a girl who was also of mixed British and Japanese descent. It was Tomisaburo who led the memorial service which was attended by many dignitaries including the British Ambassador to Japan and the founders of the Mitsubishi Corporation. After cremation in Tokyo his ashes were interned at the Sakamoto International Cemetery in his beloved Nagasaki.

There was, however, a sad postscript to the Glover story. Tomisaburo and his wife moved into the Glover House in Nagasaki after his father's death and he led a quiet but contended life with his wife, the couple having no family. Japan's entry into World War II, however, changed all that. Despite his Japanese citizenship Tomisaburo was suspected of spying for the British and interrogated on several occasions. In 1943 his wife died and left him alone and on 26 August 1945, two weeks after the Atomic bomb had wiped out the northern half of Nagasaki while leaving the southern part including the Glover House relatively untouched, he committed suicide.

More than a hundred years after the death of Thomas Blake Glover his name is still known and respected worldwide and he is revered in the land he adopted as home for much of his life. The Glover House in Nagasaki, now a World Heritage site, is one of the most visited historical properties in Japan and at one time attracted two million visitors a year. Sadly the situation is rather different in his native land and there are reports of Japanese visitors to Scotland coming to Aberdeen to visit the house (formerly known as Braehead Cottage) which Glover had bought for his parents and which he stayed in on his visits home only to discover that the house had been allowed to deteriorate into a state of disrepair with its contents, which included furniture and artefacts from Japan, having been sold off.

Fortunately the situation in Fraserburgh is better. For the best part of three decades the Thomas Blake Glover Foundation kept the name alive from an office in the town thanks to the selfless actions of founder and chair person Anne Malcolm and her team of volunteers. In 2016 Anne was at last recognised for her amazing work with a presentation by Consul General Hajime Kitaoka, the Japanese script translating as '*Congratulations! Award by Consul General of Japan. Dear Mrs Malcolm, You have made a distinguished contribution to the promotion of mutual understanding and friendship between Scotland and Japan. I hereby would like to pay my utmost respect to you and give this award to celebrate your remarkable achievements. Hajime Kitaoka, 16 March 2016*'.

Anne Malcolm receives her award from the Japanese Consul General

The Broch also boasts a permanent and fascinating exhibition about the man and his life in the Fraserburgh Heritage Centre while at the time of writing the site of the house on Commerce Street where Glover was born, which has lain derelict for over 70 years after being struck by a German bomb during the Second World War, is being transformed into a memorial garden which will hopefully attract more visitors to Fraserburgh and expand interest in the remarkable life of the Scottish Samurai

In 2016 *Giacomo & Glover,* a play based on an idea by Anne Malcolm about a fictional meeting between the composer and the industrialist days after the disastrous premiere of the *Madame Butterfly* opera premiered.

The play was staged by the Burgesses of Guild of Aberdeen over the course of two evenings at the Town House in Aberdeen with an invited audience that included Lord Provost Barney Crockett and his wife and the Honorary Italian Consul to Aberdeen. For further information on the play and staging rights contact the writer at mikegibb32@outlook.com.

For anyone interested in finding out more about the fascinating life of Thomas Blake Glover there are a number of excellent books about the man including the following:

Scottish Samurai: Thomas Blake Glover by Alexander McKay (Canongate Books)

Blossom & Frost by Brian Burke-Gaffney

The Pure Land by Alan Spence (Canongate Books)

At the Edge of the Empire: The Life of Thomas Blake Glover by Michael Gardiner (Birlinn Books)

The cast of the play (Act One) with writer Mike Gibb and Lord Provost Barney Crockett

And the cast of Act Two

Provost Alexander Nicol
(1812- 1880

The Forgotten philanthropist

In 1272 Richard Cementarius, an architect who designed the old Brig o' Balgownie and the tower at Drum Castle, was elected as the first Provost of Aberdeen. Through the centuries that have followed some three hundred men, and in recent times a handful of women, have held the prestigious post of Provost or, latterly, Lord Provost of the City.

A few have been honoured by having major road arteries named after them such as Provosts Rust, Fraser and Watt while the house of Provost Skene remains one of few historic buildings that didn't fall foul to the madness of sixties architects.

Provost Alexander Nicol is not a name that would mean a great deal to the average Aberdonian and in truth there wasn't a great deal about his years in office, which ran from 1866 to 1869, that would give his memory longevity. However, what he subsequently achieved, spurred on by his experiences as Lord Provost, is well worthy of attention and acclaim.

Alexander Nicol was born in Aberdeen on 18 October 1812 the son of Peter Nicol and Anne Jaffrey and went on to become a successful ship owner. On 10 August 1845 he married Mary Arbuthnott, a lassie from Peterhead six years his junior, but tragically less than a year after the wedding Mary died. Nicol married again in 1855 to Jane Chalmers and they had four children although tragedy again struck when one of them, Charles Alexander, died shortly after his third birthday.

Nicol was elected as Provost in 1866 having previously served as a councillor. During his term in office he became increasingly concerned by the living conditions of the city's poorest residents and vowed to do something about it as soon as has he had handed back his chain of office. And so, on 10 March 1870 Nicol gathered with a group of other local businessmen with philanthropic tendencies and founded the Association for Improving the Condition of the Poor with an aim to *'help the poor to help themselves. Foster among them habits of economy, industry and cleanliness, and consequently sentiments of independence and self respect'*. The charity subsequently changed its name in 1973 to Voluntary Services Aberdeen and on 10 March 2020 the VSA celebrated its 150th anniversary.

But back in 1870 the founders realised that their new Association required a figure head in order to capture the imagination of the public at large and an approach was made to Queen Victoria who agreed to be their patron; suddenly the Association was off and running. To Nicol the greatest blight on Aberdeen was the slums where large numbers of people, often in poor health and underfed, were crowded into disgusting and unsanitary conditions. And the worst of these were the Denburn slums, described as *'the greatest nuisance in the city'*.

Queen Victoria, first patron of the Association

The Den burn rises in Kingswells and flows east through the Den of Maidencraig, curves around Woodend Hospital and passes through the Rubislaw and Gilcomston areas before flowing in Aberdeen Harbour six miles from its source. In 1840 to make way for the rail line travelling north culverts were installed directing the waters through the city centre.

The 19ᵗʰ Century Denburn slums

Those living in slum housing on the banks of the burn were forced to use it to wash themselves and their clothes but unfortunately the waterway was also a receptacle for industrial and human waste. For that reason it wasn't any great surprise that disease was rife amongst those living in those houses which were totally devoid of any toilet facilities with the families using a large zinc pail which was emptied on a communal midden, a haven for flies and fleas, behind the houses. In a world where every newly built home seems to have more bathrooms than occupants it would be totally impossible for people today to fathom the crammed conditions that families lived in back then. 'You mean that they had to share a toilet? What, they didn't have a toilet at all!' would be the reaction of the average 21st Century teenager.

Amongst the VSA archives there is a report from the 1870's which states that *'A family of eight persons inhabit a single room only 14ft v 13ft. They consist of father and mother, with five of a family, from twenty eight years old down to ten. The oldest, a daughter has three illegitimate children, one of whom is with her. How can it be expected that any good can come of these poor children?'*

That was just one example of the conditions in which many, many families were living at that time. It was clear that a fledgling charity could not possibly tackle a problem of that scale, a crisis that required a concentrated effort from the council to provide new homes, and instead the Association endeavoured to help with short term assistance for families, providing temporary financial support when things were at their worst and endeavouring to find employment for those fit, and willing, to work. To those ends they quickly recruited an army of 500 people with a benevolent disposition each of whom took on the task of visiting and supporting those most in need and to build up a relationship *'through gentle speech and behaviour, kindly inquiry and interest and advice of a practical sort'* and they undoubtedly made a huge difference to the lives of the unfortunate families they engaged with.

While still relatively in its infancy the Association was confronted by a major challenge in the winter of 1874/75 which was so severe that many men working as labourers found themselves out of work and virtually destitute. While handouts were a short term solution the charity realised that they really needed to do something more. They subsequently reported in their annual report that *'Every able-bodied man who presented himself at the office of the Association during the continuance of the storm was supplied with a pick-axe and a spade and a card from the Association bearing the holder's name and rate of remuneration to be given. With these he was sent out to offer his services to householders, and in a day or two the applications by households requiring such a service were so numerous that they could with difficulty be attended to with the number of men available'.*

The men were utilised to clear the streets and footpaths of snow while the Association also rented premises in West North Street which were utilised for the cutting of firewood. It proved such a success that the workshop was retained and became a permanent part of the charity's work for the next forty years. As a consequence of the success of the scheme, when the weather improved 51 men had found permanent employment while another 32 remained at the workshop.

Another of the new Association's core policies was to try to achieve temperance not an easy task in a city which in the later part of the 19th Century had a population of around 80,000 and which boasted, if that is the right word, over 200 public houses. What made the situation for those living in poverty worse is that many of these bars were housed in the area that was walking, or perhaps more accurately staggering, distance of the Denburn slums. The Lemon Tree Tavern, the Prince of Wales, Ma Cameron's, the Well o' Spa, the Saltoun Arms, Ye Old Frigate and countless others were all in the city centre and gladly opened their doors wide to working men.

At that time most of those in employment would have worked a six day week with those particularly fortunate knocking off at lunchtime on a Saturday. Either way their final task at the end of their working week was to pick up their wages before heading straight for the nearest watering hole where the cheerful proprietor was ready and willing to help them dispose of the contents of the wage packet, money that was often desperately needed at home to feed undernourished children. But there was another and even darker side to the problem of drink. While several 'half and a' wee half'' would turn many of the drinkers into jovial gents who enjoyed a joke and the chance to sing songs, usually extolling the virtues of their native city or country, for others inebriation had quite the opposite effect and domestic violence was rife on a Saturday night with children living in

The Lemon Tree, the Lang Bar & the Charlotte Street Tavern

fear of their father returning home and many women given a Seterday black eye The Association were particularly concerned with the plight of children and in 1889 a scheme was adopted to provide help in a relatively simple but highly effective way with the launching of 'Fresh Air Fortnight'. Readers of a certain age will no doubt remember back to their childhood when their failure to close a door while leaving any room in the house would be greeted with a parental reprimand 'what do you think this is? Fresh air fortnight!' This remark would no doubt be met with a response which combined a loud sigh with a shrug of the shoulders, signifying disinterest and mystification as to just what Mater or Pater were talking about.

The former Unitarian Church on Skene Street Aberdeen

The idea was the brainchild of the Reverend Alexander Webster a man born in Oldmedrum in 1840 but who spent half of his life as a Minister with the Unitarian Church in the south of Scotland. While in Aberdeen, however, during a spell from 1895 to 1901 he was the driving force behind an impressive new Church building on Skene Street, close to its junction with Rosemount Viaduct. Indeed through extensive fund raising tours in both the UK and the USA Webster was able to secure almost a quarter of the £7370 that the building and its contents cost and the Church was opened to its steadily increasing congregation in July 1906. The Unitarian Church remained there until 1987 when it swapped properties with Jehovah's Witness who had a smaller property in nearby Skene Terrace and to this day 'Webster's kirk' is used by the faithful under the name of the Kingdom Hall.

But Webster was not only a Minister of the Church but a fervent and radical socialist and key member of the Aberdeen Labour Party and became known for holding rallies on the City's Broad Hill which would attract hundreds to listen to the Minister's Christian and Socialist beliefs. He also got involved with various groups with political left wing tendencies eventually becoming Vice President of the Scottish Labour Party, a group established by Keir Hardie.

James Keir Hardie was born in Newhouse in Lanarkshire in 1856 and by 1863, aged just seven, he had begun his working life before going 'down pit' in the local coal mines as a ten year old. With a background in preaching he was a powerful public speaker and a spokesman for the miners, subsequently leading strikes in both Lanarkshire and Ayrshire.

Having taken a job in journalism he became convinced that Gladstone's Liberal Party weren't doing sufficient for the workers and stood for Parliament in 1888 before, later that year, forming the Scottish Labour Party. Under an Independent banner he was elected to the seat of West Ham South in 1892 and the following year helped to establish a U.K. wide Labour Party.

He returned to Parliament as the representative for Merthyr Tydfil in South Wales and was elected as the Labour Party's first Westminster Leader in 1906. He subsequently stood aside to concentrate on supporting causes such as Women's Suffrage and opposition to World

War I and died in 1915 while endeavouring to organise a pacifist general strike. To this day he is regarded as the father of the Labour movement and was undoubtedly a man that Alexander Webster, with his strong socialist principles, would have greatly admired.

Keir Hardie making one of his famous speeches

When Webster returned to the North East in 1884 after a spell preaching at a Unitarian Church in Glasgow he was dismayed by the living conditions for many in the city and in particular for the underfed children who ran around barefoot and dressed in rags and who never had the chance to breath clean air or to see a blade of grass. His aim was to give as many of them as possible the opportunity to taste the better things in life by taking them out of their environment for at least a brief period of time.

Through the Fresh Air Fortnight scheme each and every child was given a bath, a somewhat rare experience for most of them, before being kitted out in new apparel. A label was then attached with their name and destination and they were ready for the great venture; and an adventure it undoubtedly was. It is unlikely that any of them had ever been on a train despite the fact that they were well used to seeing large locomotives, belching out sooty smoke, passing their houses on a regular basis. It must also have been mesmerising for the kids to look out of the carriage windows to see farm lands and cows and sheep and so much more for the very first time in their lives.

Rev. Webster approached the North of Scotland Railway Company and successfully negotiated a special rate of ten pence and a ha'penny (roughly 4 pence in current currency) per child. That paid for their return journey with the train guards being given the somewhat demanding task of ensuring that the correct child was deposited at the desired destination as none of the children would have had a clue where they were headed.

For two whole weeks these kids ran about and played in clean, fresh air while also eating healthy food in plentiful quantities. Not surprisingly, the scheme proved to be hugely popular and in its first year alone 555 children from the worst of the Aberdeen slums took part. Once the scheme was well established a permanent home was secured in the form of Linn Moor House at Peterculter. It may have only been six miles from Aberdeen but for the children going there it must have seemed like a trip to the moon.

When it opened in 1908 Linn Moor was able to accommodate fifty children at a time with this number being increased the following year to seventy. The centre's heyday stretched on until 1939 while during the war years it was used for evacuees. Although it continued after the war, changes in circumstances saw a reduction in demand and eventually 74 years after it had been launched Fresh Air Fortnight was wound up. But to this day Linn Moor is still a facility operated by the VSA, now as a residential school for disabled children and those with learning difficulties, a lasting testament to the Rev. Alexander Webster who died in Cults in 1918. His contribution to life in Aberdeen was recognised in early 2019 when a Civic Reception hosted by the Lord Provost Barney Crockett was held in the Town House to mark the 100th anniversary of his death.

Children playing at Linn Moor during Fresh Air Fortnight

While the establishment of the Fresh Air Fortnight scheme was one of the Association's greatest and certainly most high profile achievements, on a day to day basis they were also helping individuals who found themselves in dire straits. Cases like Elizabeth Hutcheon who, aged 46, was suddenly widowed when her husband was drowned at sea in 1897. She was left living at 21 Albion Street Aberdeen with four children all under the age of twelve and without the intervention of the Association would have been rendered destitute. The charity gave her a weekly allowance to enable her to heat the house and provide sustenance to her family until an insurance pay out materialised. Just one small example of how the charity was to hand when desperately needed.

In its early days in particular the Association must have been greatly encouraged when they saw people they had aided reciprocating by helping others even less fortunate. There is a mention in an early Annual Report of a '*worthy woman, who has to toil for herself and her children along the blank edge of sheer poverty, performing all the kindest offices of friendship for her more destitute neighbours – a very blessing to them in trouble and sickness*' and of '*a woman deserted by her husband who has to support a young family, and who lives in one of the most neglected lanes of the city, is to all appearances the unpaid nurse of her infirm neighbours. She has applied to the Association for others, but never herself.*'

Another excellent example of the 'poor helping the poor' was 'The Fiddler', a well known local worthy. He was to be found entertaining passers-by in St. Nicholas Square until the tent in which he lived was destroyed by fire together with all his worldly possessions including his precious fiddle. With no other source of income he would have starved if the charity hadn't stepped in and bought him a new fiddle. He rewarded their generosity by donating part of his takings to the Association for many years thereafter. Over the first thirty years of its existence the Association had encountered countless cases where individuals required a helping hand but in 1904 it suddenly found itself confronted with a far larger problem.

In 1824 Thomas Bannerman, a Dean of Guild and a well known businessman in the Aberdeen area, established a textile mill near the Queens Links on Cotton Street. It was named the Banner Mill and provided work for hundreds of local people courtesy of a 100,000 spindles. In 1850 the premises were sold to Robinson, Crum and Co. Ltd who continued to produce textiles until the early part of the 20th Century.

In February 1904 Aberdeen was once again in the grip of a particular harsh winter and the work force daily had to tramp through deep snow to get to the Mill. On arriving one morning they were surprised to find that the large metal gates were closed and padlocked and all too soon they realised that the rumours that had been circulating for sometime about the business being in financial difficulties were true. Overnight the owners had simply decided to cease trading and to close the Mill.

Banner Mill Works in the 19th Century

Suddenly 400 people were unemployed, the majority of them women. This wasn't because females were necessarily better than the men at the tasks although they were certainly their equal; no, the reason that woman were employed was that they could be paid half a man's wage. But although most of those abruptly out of work were women many of them were the chief and, in some instances, sole bread winner in the family and without the intervention of the Association it is possible that people may have starved or frozen to death.

The Association recognised the severity of the situation and a committee was immediately set up to address the problem. When it became obvious that the Mill could not be saved as a going concern they established, with the support of the Aberdeen Union of Women Workers, a drop-in centre for the former employees in premises they secured in the Gallowgate. They offered these people free meals and grants to cover expenses such as rent while they also began training courses teaching new skills as well as paying for outfits or uniforms that might be required if alternate sources of employment could be found.

The Gallowgate in Aberdeen

The efforts of the Association were quite outstanding with 36 of the women placed in employment at the Stanley Cotton Mills and work as domestic servants was found for a similar number all within a remarkably short time of Banner Mill closing. Many of the other women began working at the Aberdeen Comb Works and in other local factories in the city, some at fish curing houses in the harbour area while others, thanks to the training that had been given, began labour in gardens or on farms. Within six weeks of the Mill closing every single one of the 400 former employees had been found alternate employment and the crisis was overcome. And all for the princely sum of £161.9s.6d.

A couple of decades later the Association addressed another problem in that same area of Aberdeen albeit a very different one. In an era where few people could afford to travel out with the city on holiday Aberdeen Beach was hugely popular. The sheer size of many of the families meant that children going missing at the seaside was a major problem. In 1927 the charity decided to address this issue by erecting a tent at the Beach manned by volunteers where lost children could be looked after until they were reclaimed.

It says a great deal not only about the volume of beach goers but equally about the lack of diligence of the parents that during the first month the tent was in operation 96 children were reunited with their owners. The following year the tent was folded up and a permanent beach shelter built in its place.

But there were far bigger challenges for the Association during the Twenties when things were clearly not roaring in Aberdeen. The winter of 1921/22 was particularly cold and severe (yes again) and applications to the charity for help rose dramatically from the previous year's level of 990 to 8216, leaving the Association reeling and barely able to cope. In fact had they not joined forces with the Parish Council they might have buckled under the deluge but together the organisations rose to the challenge.

The conditions which caused this situation were more economic than meteorological in nature with the country in the grip of the Great Depression that followed on from the First World War and which saw mass unemployment, not just in the manual workers who the Association had long supported but also amongst the skilled workforce. By 1933 there were an estimated 14,000 men and women unemployed in the City.

Fortunately the partnership between the two organisations proved highly successful with the groups neatly complementing each other. The criteria that the Parish Council established for receipt of grant monies was quite stringent and the Association were often able to step in and offer assistance to people who had been turned away by the sister organisation.

The Great Depression of the 1920's and 30's

In 1922 the Association again came up with an inspired scheme, one which they called the 'Bairns Boot and Clothing Fund'. In this day and age the average teenager's wardrobe can probably boast half a dozen pairs of trainers some of which will never see the light of day again, not because they are worn out but simply because they have the wrong colour of tick or triple stripe logo or are last year's model. A hundred years ago things were rather different.

Kids had one pair of footwear and when those wore out the children went barefoot. Mindful that it was clearly detrimental to bairns' health to tramp around shoeless in cold days the Association set about addressing the problem. Once news of the scheme surfaced the charity found themselves swamped with up to a hundred requests a week and as funds were not inexhaustible they employed their own shoemaker during the winter months to repair the footwear that could be salvaged, an early example of the British Ministry of Information's slogan during the Second World War of 'make good and mend'.

But it wasn't just children that were in need of such basic apparel and in the Association's Annual Report for 1925 it was revealed that the shoemaker they had employed had been able to supply 1100 pairs of boots and shoes for men and women to wear when heading to work. The situation was also helped by the generous acts of individuals such as a gentleman by the name of Mr. A.C. Little who ran an apparel shop under his own name at 105 Union Street and who donated 300 pairs of boots and shoes for the charity to distribute.

Although the Great Depression was clearly the most difficult situation that the Association and, in its more modern guise the VSA, has had to deal with, the charity has successfully navigated through two World Wars, two Pandemics and many more difficult periods without ever having failed to rise to the challenge. One hundred and fifty years after its inception the VSA is an organisation that is known and respected far beyond the boundaries of its native city, helping vulnerable children and adults in so many different ways.

Alexander Nicol would be justifiably proud of the charitable organisation that he helped to create. Sadly he died in Peterculter a mere ten years after the charity had been founded and his legacy is marked by no more than a simple granite cross at his grave in Old Machar Cemetery. But it is never too late to remedy that situation; after all Provost Nicol Drive does have a rather nice ring to it.

Provost Alexander Nicol's grave at Old Machar Cemetery

VSA
THE PRIDE OF ABERDEEN

To commemorate the 150th anniversary a short play was commissioned by the charity with the support of Heritage Scotland. Performed by actors Carolyn Johnston, Brian McDonald and Michelle Bruce and with music provided by Mairi Paton Warren, it was filmed by Pink Sphynx Media and can now be viewed on the 'Our Heritage' page of the charity's website at https://heritage.vsa.org.uk/.

Reverend James Ramsay
(1733-1789)

'The single most important influence
in the abolition of the slave trade'

When, at some future date, people look back at the year 2020 they will remember one thing only. The Pandemic that directly affected more or less every country in every corner of the world. And yet there was another event arising for a single incident in Minneapolis in the shape of the killing of George Floyd by a Policeman in a botched arrest which quite rightly drew worldwide condemnation and remonstration.

Unfortunately, as so often happens with protest movements of all kinds, the central premise of complaint got lost along the way as attention veered from the sad demise of Floyd and began to be focused on somewhat more ancient history in the form of the slave trade.

No one can fail to accept that such a practice was totally abhorrent but the protesters, in a wave of self righteous indignation, decided to direct their collective ire on inanimate objects, statues that had stood for centuries totally unnoticed by everyone with the exception of pigeons who regarded them as a spot to rest and defecate.

If the subject of slavery is to take centre stage then surely the best means of addressing the evils of the past isn't to dump large blocks of granite into waterways but to publicise the actions of the few, the brave few, who stood tall in the face of provocation and at great risk to their personal safety in order to see the evil practice abolished. Men who are now largely sadly forgotten; men like the Reverend James Ramsay from Fraserburgh.

For such a small Scottish fishing town – even now in the 21st Century it only has a population of 13,000 – it can boast a remarkable number of famous sons as even a cursory read of this book will reveal. But back in 1733 when James Ramsay was born on 25 July there were little more than 2000 'Brochers'. Having left school he was offered an apprenticeship but not by the local joiner or plumber but instead by a surgeon. It is a rather frightening thought that a patient arrived for surgery only to be informed by the boss man that he was a bit busy but the apprentice would sort them out.

Clearly his experiences whetted his appetite for a career in the medical profession as in 1750 aged 17 James headed for Aberdeen University and within three years had obtained an M.A. degree from King's College. After a further spell of study in Aberdeen and subsequently in London with esteemed practitioner Dr. George Macaulay, Ramsay joined the Navy. Perhaps the sea had always been in his blood as his father William Ramsay worked as a ship's carpenter.

He was appointed surgeon aboard *HMS Arundel*, a warship built at Chichester in 1746, with Ramsay responsible for the health of the 160 members of the crew. The Royal Navy vessel was sent to patrol around British dependencies in the West Indies and a short time after taking up the commission an event occurred that changed the life of not only James Ramsay but, it could certainly be argued, countless others.

In 1750 the Arundel encountered a British slave ship, the *Swift*, which was in distress having been boarded on its journey to Barbados by a French privateer vessel. On discovering that there was an outbreak of dysentery on the *Swift* the boarders had taken only the healthy slaves leaving behind a hundred men and women in desperate straits. Ramsay boarded the vessel and was truly appalled by the conditions in which the slaves were being transported and so moved that when he returned to the *Arundel* he was in such a perplexed state that he fell and broke a thigh bone.

He never totally recovered from that accident, walking with a pronounced limp for the rest of his life, and two years later he was discharged from the Navy as being unfit for service.

As a young boy Ramsay had always wanted to become a Minister of the Church but realised that with his father's meagre earnings it was not a road that he could afford to follow. In returning to Britain in 1761, however, he took Holy Orders and by November of that year had been ordained by the Bishop of London. What he had witnessed aboard the *Swift* still haunted him and he asked to be sent to the Caribbean in the hope that he could work amongst the slaves. He ended up on the island of St. Christopher.

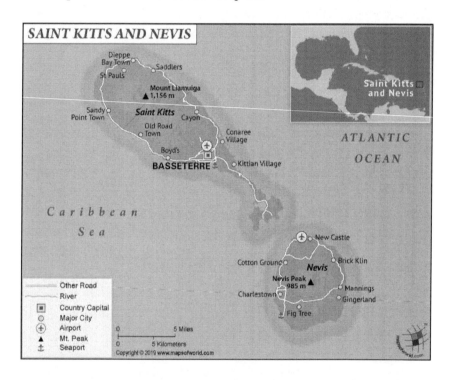

St. Christopher, or St. Kitts as it is now referred to, is a small island in what, back in jolly colonial days, was known as the British West Indies. Discovered by Christopher Columbus in 1493 the English established a settlement there in 1623 followed two years later by the French. In a rare demonstration of entente cordiale, bearing in mind that for centuries those two countries had been knocking lumps out of each other in a series of pointless wars, the English and French teamed up for the sole purpose of massacring the local Kalinago peoples who had been living a nice peaceful existence until the Europeans arrived and decided to 'civilise' them.

Having carved up St. Kitts and the neighbouring Nevis Island between them, the English and French then set their collective minds to the most important issue; how they could exploit the island with its clement climate to make the most money. Initially they grew tobacco until the Americans in Virginia found they could produce it cheaper and the bottom fell out of the market as far as the West Indies were concerned.

Before long, however, the joint rulers of the islands had come up with an alternative – sugar. It was relatively cheap to produce although labour intensive and that is where slaves came into play. The plantation owners needed inexpensive labour to maximise profits and what was even better was a workforce that didn't need to be paid at all. Having people that could be worked to death, literally in many cases, without dipping into their collective pockets provided them with sugar cane and able bodied workers.

Slavery may not be the world's oldest profession but it is close. It was to be found in Mesopotamia as long ago at 3500 BC and anyone who has watched the TV mini-series like *Rome* and *Spartacus* will be well aware of how widespread and important it was to the way of life in Roman times. It is, however, the era of the African slave that caused the most controversy.

The trade had many forms although in the 18th and early 19th century it primarily involved people being rounded up in the West of Africa and then shipped to the New World, America and the Caribbean Islands, a sea voyage of more than 4000 miles. For Britain it was one leg of a highly lucrative business known as the triangular route accounting for 80% of all overseas income. British goods were exported to Africa, slaves loaded up in the cargo hold and taken to the Caribbean and America where they were replaced with sugar, cotton and tobacco before the ship returned home.

The number of slaves who were transported in this way was astronomical with some estimates putting it as high as 20 million; if that figure is correct then up to 3 million men, women and children would have perished in the crossing as a direct consequence of the appalling crowded conditions, a shortage of edible food and the prevalence of disease, as a result of which the ships became known as 'tumberois' or floating tombs.

What made the journey even more horrific for the slaves was their innate terror of the sea and the fact that if they died at sea their bodies would simply be thrown overboard which they believed meant that they went straight to hell. Mind you it is doubtful if hell could have been any worse than the life they were suffering on the ships.

The crowded conditions on a ship transporting slaves

The slaves who arrived in the likes of St. Kitts were then bought by local plantation owners for about £60 each and immediately put to work for sixteen hours a day, being wakened at 4 am to commence their daily tasks. The difficulties that they faced were countless and insurmountable although at the top of the list was the fact that the owners viewed them as 'sub-human' and as a result had no hesitation in treating them in the most barbaric way, unmoved and unconcerned by the suffering they inflicted.

It was against this backdrop that the Rev. Ramsay arrived on St. Christopher originally taking up a post at St. John's Church in Capisterre before transferring the following year to Christ Church in Nichola Town. Quite soon he began welcoming all to the church, hopeful of converting the slaves to Christianity, a move that was not well received by the plantation owners who were no doubt concerned that the Minister might provide their workers with not only belief but, of more concern, with hope. Indeed some of the island's leading lights urged whites to boycott Ramsay's church on the grounds that the man was '*fit company only for blacks*'.

At the same time the owners were more than happy to accept his advice and treatment in the event of illness, James calling on his medical background to help those in need irrespective of colour. And the slaves were grateful for his attention although more often it was their mistreatment rather than just common ailments that laid them low. Through visiting the plantations more or less daily he witnessed not only the inhuman conditions in which the slaves had to live and work but the disgusting treatment of them. The bull whip was carried by every overseer and administered indiscriminately for the slightest infringement of the rules, '*cutting out flakes of skin and flesh with every strike*' as Ramsay later recalled while something as simple as breaking a sugar cane could result in a slave being cut to ribbons by a cutlass. Ramsay described a regime where it was '*in the master's power to render his slaves' lives miserable every hour by a thousand*

nameless stratagems' and was equally concerned by a situation whereby slave
girls were '*sacrificed to the lust of white men, in some instances their own fathers*'. But the more that the Minister highlighted the plight of the slaves, bringing the matter to the attention of the local government, the more he fell afoul of their masters and he was regularly and repeatedly subject to antagonism and personal attacks by men who were clearly concerned that their source of free labour would dry up and which would consequently hit them where it hurt most; in their pockets.

Slaves working in the cane fields watched by the boss man with the ever ready bull whip

Although Ramsay was generally disliked by the white settlers everyone didn't follow that road and he began courting Rebecca

Akers, daughter of plantation and slave owner Edmund Akers, and the couple married, subsequently having four children.

Having secured the slaves to harvest the sugar cane, the plantation owners set about building processing plants and refineries on St. Kitts. It is fair to say that Health and Safety were not matters of great concern to the plantation owners and accidents were frequent and often severe with Ramsay on one occasion being prevented from attending to a man who had caught his arm in a grinding machine, the owner preferring to allow the slave to bleed to death in excruciating pain.

In his dual role of tending to spiritual and physical well-being he was constantly in demand and the arrival of a ship with small pox saw him going on board to try and assist those in distress. He would clearly have taken precautions, including no doubt wearing a mask, to avoid catching the disease himself but unfortunately omitted to take account of the fact that the highly contagious virus could cling to clothing. As a result he brought it home infecting his only son who tragically died as a result.

After the best part of two decades on the island the Rev. Ramsay was worn down by the work and the animosity that greeted him daily. As a result when an invitation was received from Sir Charles Middleton to spend time with him and his wife back in Britain he happily accepted and in 1780 he took up the post of vicar at the local church at Teston near Maidstone in Kent. But if the plantation owners on the Caribbean Island thought that they had won a moral victory by ridding themselves of their chief critic, history would show that they were sadly misguided.

Sir Charles Middleton was a fellow Scot, having been born in Leith, and a friend of Ramsay from his Royal Navy days, both having served on *HMS Arundel*. During an illustrious although on occasions overly colourful naval career (he was demoted on one occasion for striking a fellow sailor) he commanded a vessel during the Seven Year War in

America and distinguished himself while on duty in the West Indies capturing sixteen French vessels and several ships belonging to privateers.

The Church at Teston

When he married Margaret Gambier in 1761 he turned his back on the sea and donned the mantle of country gentleman, farming lands near Teston. However when the American War of Independence broke out he was appointed Comptroller of the Navy, a post he held for 12 years being created a Baronet in the process. The next change of direction came in 1784 when Sir Charles was elected as Member of Parliament for Rochester and remained at Westminster for six years although during that period he was also promoted to Rear Admiral. Several naval promotions followed before finally, at the age of 80, he was made First Lord of the Admiralty.

But it wasn't just a naval career that Ramsay and Middleton had in common as the later was influenced by his friend's anti-slavery views as was Lady Margaret Middleton. While tempted to take up the reins himself, Middleton was conscious that it would be a long hard struggle to get any legislation outlawing slavery through the House of Commons and felt that the fight should be led by a younger man. He subsequently persuaded fellow MP William Wilberforce to get involved and in the process introduced Wilberforce to Ramsay.

Barham Court the Middleton's home

It was around that time that James Ramsay truly made his mark by producing a pamphlet titled *'An Essay on the Treatment and Conversion of African Slaves in the British Sugar Colonies'*. The rather long winded title was forced on him by friends who steered him away from an alternate title he preferred on the grounds that it was too controversial and inflammatory. The work was well received by those with an interest in the subject but could have been *'swallowed up in the gulf of oblivion'* as the author put it had those opposed to its content not objected so vociferously.

One man even challenged Ramsay to a duel and the fuss they created had the effect of stirring up interest in the work and opening the eyes of sections of the British public ignorant of the repugnant practice.

Eventually the booklet was described in The Dictionary of National Biography as *'The single most important influence in the abolition of the slave trade'.*

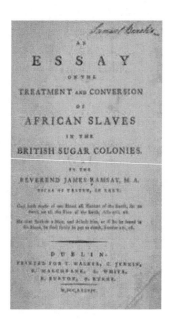

With Lady Margaret Middleton firmly on board the abolitionists began to grow in strength and numbers and the leading lights of the movement including the Bishop of Chester and Thomas Clarkson regularly met in the Middleton's palatial home of Barham Court. Ramsay was so encouraged by support emanating from so many influential people that he produced a second written work which, believe it or not, had an even less snappy title than its predecessor in the form of *'An Inquiry into the Effects of Putting a Stop to the African Slave Trade: And of Granting Liberty to the Slaves in the British Sugar Colonies'.*

By this stage Ramsay was beginning to mix with elevated company including William Pitt the Younger who had just been elected to the office of Prime Minister at the tender age of 24, the youngest person ever to hold that role. His appointment led to a great deal of mockery including a poem which became famous and may have prompted the TV comedy series *Black Adder* to depict Pitt as a spotty faced school kid.

> *Above the rest, majestically great,*
> *Behold the infant Atlas of the state,*
> *The matchless miracle of modern days,*
> *In whom Britannia to the world displays*
> *A sight to make surrounding nations stare;*
> *A kingdom trusted to a school-boy's care.*

Pitt had only been a Member of Parliament for less than three years, having entered the chamber in a somewhat dubious manner by winning the 'rotten borough' seat of Appleby. When he took over the top job in December 1783 it was widely forecast that his administration wouldn't last beyond Christmas. It was in power for seventeen years.

It was while he was at Cambridge that Pitt had made the acquaintance of William Wilberforce and the friendship they forged at University continued when they both ended up in Westminster. Wilberforce, a name that will forever be associated with the abolition of slavery was born on 24 August 1759 in Hull. He was a slight, sickly child with poor eyesight but came from a wealthy family and inheritances meant that he never had to worry about money.

After a spell at Cambridge where he became interested in politics he followed his University friend William Pitt to Westminster gaining his seat at Kingston Upon Hull after parting with £8000, an enormous sum in 1780, to buy votes. Clearly politics in this country was just as murky back then. He announced that he would not be joining either of the major parties, the Tories or the Whigs, but entered the House of Commons as an Independent. As a result and despite his close relationship with Pitt, who became Prime Minister, Wilberforce never served as a Minister. It is suggested that another reason that he didn't climb the political ladder was his reputation for tardiness and living a hedonistic life style which involved gambling and late night drinking sessions at the likes of the Goostree's and Boodle's gambling club in Pall Mall.

Wilberforce changed all that, however, when during a jaunt round the hot spots of Europe he found religion and began to take life and in particular the many inequalities he witnessed seriously. And high on that list of such injustices was the evil of slavery.

William Wilberforce

Wilberforce's interest in the abolitionists' campaign was stoked by a meeting at Barham Court hosted by the Middletons with the group which became known as Testonites and which included James Ramsay in their ranks while William was also moved and inspired by the Minister's *'Essay'*. He began to raise the subject in Parliament but it proved to be a long and arduous road with many obstacles along the way.

In April 1791 he introduced a parliamentary bill and his strength of feeling for the cause was clear for all to see as Wilberforce spoke on the subject for four hours. Unfortunately the French Revolution had resulted in a conservative, with a small c, mood enveloping the Commons, a fact that was emphasised when the bill was comfortably defeated.

Undaunted, he continued his campaign with his strongly held belief in Christian principles driving him on as did the horrors that had been graphically described to him by Ramsay and others who had firsthand knowledge of the suffering of the slaves. Two years after the first bill had been defeated its successor fell by the wayside. By this time the margin had shrunk to a mere 8 votes showing how the mood was changing but a subsequent war with France, yes another one, meant that the question of abolition was placed on the back burner. By 1804, however, Wilberforce was able to see yet another bill pass all its stages in the House of Commons only for time to run out before it could be ratified in the Lords. How many poor souls spent their all too brief life in misery simply because Knights of the Realm were heading off on their summer hols?

In January 1806 Wilberforce's ally, William Pitt, died and the abolitionist used the change in leadership to cosy up to the Whig opposition party, who were more sympathetic, and with their support the Slave Trade Act was passed in 1807. It made it illegal to trade in slaves but in no way assisted those already living 'under the whip'. In any event that act proved almost impossible to enforce and it wasn't until 1833 that the Slavery Abolition Act passed through the House enjoying Royal assent in July of that year. Weeks later on 29 July Wilberforce died but had no doubt passed peacefully, content to see his life's work come to fruition. Sadly the Rev. James Ramsay was not so fortunate, dying in 1789 aged fifty six. There can be no doubt that his contribution to the abolition movement was enormous although now regrettably largely forgotten. In a testament to his legacy inventor James Watt, yet another famous Scot, said of Ramsay *'His enemies acknowledged his exemplary qualities while deploring the intemperate language of his books and the abolition of the British slave trade in 1807 probably owed more to James Ramsay's personal integrity, ethical arguments and constructive proposals than to any other influence'.*

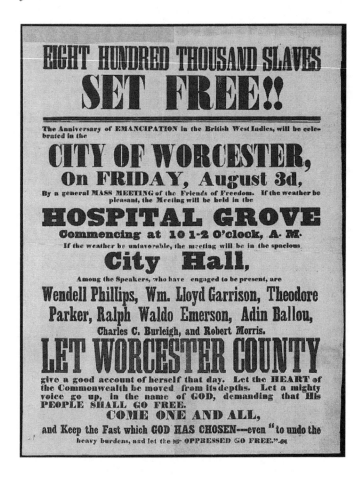

A Commemoration of the passing of the Slavery Abolition Act

The Slavery Abolition Act took effect from 1 August 1834 and in the process some 800,000 enslaved people in the British dependencies, mainly in the Caribbean and South Africa, were freed although, of course, it was more than twenty years later before their unfortunate counterparts in America were similarly released from their chains.

As Ramsay might have expected the loss of slave labour had a hugely detrimental effect on the sugar cane industry on the islands and was eventually replaced by a highly lucrative, but certainly more humane, industry. Tourism. Some of the buildings left over including a number of the extravagant villas occupied by the plantation owners were transformed into luxury hotels for visitors while many former cane fields now boast lavish villas.

Some misguided Government officials on St. Kitts at one time suggested using the sugar mill as the island's emblem but fortunately common sense prevailed and the green vervet monkey was adopted instead. The monkeys are a great feature of island life; loved by the tourists, detested by local farmers. To this day they can be seen in large numbers frolicking, free and carefree, around the same land where captive human beings once lived in abject misery.

In Memoriam

James Ramsay is remembered in his native Fraserburgh with a plaque displayed in St. Peter's Church while the park on Maconochie Road is named in his honour.

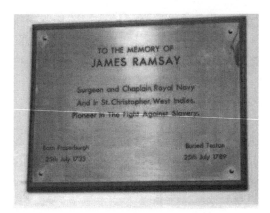

Plaque in St. Peter's Church

Official opening of the James Ramsay Park

Lewis Grassic Gibbon
(1901-1935)

A man of smeddum

Arbuthnott is a village in what was formerly known as Kincardineshire, now part of Aberdeenshire. It is sited almost exactly half way between Fordoun and Inverbervie or as the sadly missed trio of *Scotland the What?* might say 'it's affa central'. 'Blink and you'll miss it' could be a phrase that was inspired by a hamlet the size of Arbuthnott.

And yet it does have a claim to fame in boasting one of the main tourist attractions in the area in the form of a Centre created to remember the work of James Leslie Mitchell better known throughout the world as Lewis Grassic Gibbon. The writer will always be closely associated with the area of Scotland known as the Mearns and yet he wasn't originally from there nor was any of his most famous works written in that prosperous rural area.

Mitchell was born to James and Lilias Mitchell of Hillhead of Seggat farm at Auchterless, another pastoral backwater close to Turriff, on 13 February 1901 in a Scotland that was still in mourning for the death of Queen Victoria who after 64 years on the throne had passed away three weeks earlier. The family moved to Bloomfield Farm, Arbuthnott and James was enrolled at the local school, a cold two mile walk from the farmhouse, in 1908 remaining there until 1916. Among his school friends, albeit two years his junior, was Rebecca Middleton the daughter of another local crofter.

Mitchell was an avid reader and his teacher Alexander Gray was so impressed by his student that he encouraged him to attend, briefly, Mackie Academy in Stonehaven. At the age of 16, however, the lad left scholastic life and began work with the *Aberdeen Daily Journal*, a forerunner of today's P. & J.

The newspaper began life back in 1747 as the *Aberdeen Journal* and between then and the time that Mitchell joined the staff underwent numerous changes of title initially to the snappy '*The Aberdeen Journal and General Advertiser for the North of Scotland*'. Until 1901 it was a weekly publication because, according to the owners, '*the proverbial frugality, amounting almost to parsimony, of the inhabitants of this part of the kingdom, prevents any paper published more frequently than once a week, from obtaining a circulation of any considerable extent*'. When labelled in that manner is it any wonder that Aberdonians have been tarred, quite unfairly, with the epithet 'mean'?

Plaque at 5 St Mary's Place, Aberdeen

While working for the newspaper Mitchell took up residency at 5 St. Mary's Place but in 1919 he was on the move again travelling south to Glasgow to join the staff of *The Scottish Farmer* as a junior reporter. It unfortunately didn't work out for him as after only a few months he was fired for misuse of his expense fund and suffered a nervous breakdown, spending a short spell in a medical facility before enlisting in the Royal Army Service Corp. That gave the young man the opportunity to travel and see the world visiting exotic places like Egypt, Palestine, Mesopotamia (now Iraq, Turkey, Syria and Kuwait) and Persia (Iran). And yet when he eventually returned and began to write much of his work was largely centred around the hinterland just south of Aberdeen.

After his four year service he was discharged but, clearly having enjoyed military life, joined the Royal Air Force as a clerk and settled in London where he had the opportunity of trying his hand at writing. In 1924 he submitted a short story titled *Siva Plays the Game* to the publication *T.P.'s and Cassell's Weekly* and was delighted that not only was it printed but won first prize in their short story completion.

Extract from the T.P.'s and Cassell's Weekly

A year on there was another major event in his life when a chance meeting reunited him with former school friend Rebecca Middleton and after a short courtship the couple married in Fulham Register Office. They settled in Welwyn Garden City and subsequently had two children together, Rhea and Daryll, although the first baby did not arrive until after Rebecca took seriously ill while suffering a miscarriage, an event that had a lifelong traumatic effect on her husband.

No doubt encouraged by his success with his short story Mitchell began work on a book *Hanno or the Future of Exploration* which was published 1928 and a year later he submitted a short story titled *For Ten's Sake* to *The Cornhill* magazine. Having ceased publication in 1975 *The Cornhill* is now long forgotten but in its day it was a prestigious publication. Established in 1859 as a 'Victorian magazine and literary journal' by George Murray Smith and named after the London thoroughfare where it was published, it was established to try and attract away the readership of a similar publication called *All the Year Round* which was edited by Charles Dickens. William Makepeace Thackeray, Dickens great literary rival of the period, was appointed as Editor and under Thackeray's tutorship circulation of *The Cornhill* rose to 110,000 copies although that dropped dramatically when he left his post.

Nevertheless the magazine was still able to attract the cream of the literary world anxious to announce their latest work by having it serialised in the monthly publication and over the years the likes of Thomas Hardy's *Far From the Madding Crowd, Tithonus* by Alfred Tennyson and several books by Henry James were to be found within its pages. Mitchell, still a young and relatively inexperienced writer, must have been thrilled to see his short stories sitting cheek by jowl alongside such classics.

When in 1929 Mitchell found himself discharged from the RAF and with a baby on the way he took the brave decision to begin writing on a full time basis and over the following five years he produced many written works. It began with the publication in 1930 of his first novel *Stained Radiance: A Fictionist's Prelude* in which he introduced readers to a strong female lead character, a forerunner of his future work. Indeed the main character of Thea Mayven bears a striking resemblance to Mitchell's most famous literary creation, Chris Guthrie. The book follows the adventures of Mayven as she moves from the Mearns to London and gets involved with a young former Air Force clerk and would be writer, a theme with strong echoes of the author's own tale.

During the early part of the 1930's Mitchell was prolific with four published works and displayed his versatility with *Three Go Back* which was a million miles and 25000 years distant from the Mearns being a tale of time travel by an airship to a much earlier period of history. The era also saw the publication of *The Calends of Cairo* which boasted a foreword by H.G. Wells, famed for novels such as *War of the Worlds* and *The Time Machine,* in the form of two letters he had sent Mitchell declaring that it was a 'very good story'.

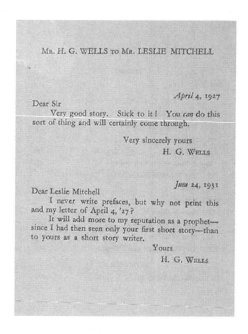

MR. H. G. WELLS TO MR. LESLIE MITCHELL

April 4, 1927

Dear Sir
    Very good story. Stick to it! You *can* do this sort of thing and will certainly come through.

Very sincerely yours
H. G. WELLS

June 24, 1931

Dear Leslie Mitchell
    I never write prefaces, but why not print this and my letter of April 4, '27?
    It will add more to my reputation as a prophet—since I had then seen only your first short story—than to yours as a short story writer.

Yours
H. G. WELLS

H. G Wells letters to Mitchell

But it was in 1932 that James Leslie Mitchell wrote the book that was destined to cement his place in history although he did so under the pen name of Lewis Grassic Gibbon. The work in question was of course *Sunset Song.*

In 2005 the Edinburgh Book Festival ran a competition to find Scotland's best book through a public vote and out on top came *Sunset Song,* a feat that it repeated eleven years later when BBC Scotland ran a similar poll. On both occasions it came in ahead of famous literary works such as Alasdair Gray's *Lanark,* Muriel

Spark's *The Prime of Miss Jean Brodie*, Ian Banks' *The Wasp Factory* and John Buchan's *Thirty Nine Steps*. Amongst those that voted for it was Scotland's First Minister Nicola Sturgeon who reinforced her love for the book by editing a recent new edition.

On the surface it would appear to be little more than the story of Chris Guthrie, a young girl with great grit and determination to face and overcome life's trials and tribulations. In her case these are thrown at her in legions from a domineering and abusive father, a suicidal mother and a husband sent to the front in the First World War and shot for desertion when he decides to leave the trenches to return home.

But dig deeper and it becomes obvious that through his depiction of the fictional Kinraddie the author is providing an examination of the changing face of Scotland during the early part of the 20th century and in particular, the sounding of the death knell of the small crofts, being replaced by the large profitable farms that now dominate the fertile lands of the Mearns. He also focuses on the disappearance of the faithful work horse as the era of mechanisation begins to alter the landscape forever.

The book doesn't just owe its fame to the printed word as some fifty years ago there was a television first; BBC Scotland recorded in colour what would now be referred to as a mini-series. They brought together a number of well known Scottish faces such as Vivien Hielbron, Paul Young, Andrew Keir and Roddy McMillan and the six part series was so well received that in the eighties the Beeb returned to Gibbon's work to record the other two parts of what became known as *A Scots Quair*.

Scottish actor Alastair Cording clearly saw the dramatic potential of the source material and set about creating a stage script of *Sunset Song*. Other playwrights followed on that same path, but Cording's remains the definitive version. One of the most famous adaption's of it for the stage was created in 1993 by the Tag Theatre Company, the production arm of Glasgow's famous Citizens Theatre. Not content with just doing *Sunset Song* they set to work on bringing all three parts of the trilogy to stage.

The rather tame cover of the controversial book

Music became an important part of those productions and singer/ songwriter Dougie MacLean was appointed as musical director. Perthshire born and based, MacLean has produced a host of critically acclaimed albums that includes a CD of music from *Sunset Song* but will always be best remembered as the writer of Scotland's alternate anthem, the wonderful *Caledonia,* written when he was exiled in Australia and homesick.

DOUGIE MACLEAN

Sunset Song

Instrumental Musical Themes Commissioned for
TAG Theatre Company's Production of "A SCOT'S QUAIR"–
a Trilogy by Lewis Grassic Gibbon (Sunset Song, Cloud Howe, Grey Granite)

Over the years Gibbon's book has been regularly and repeatedly staged and in 2008 it played a major part in the history of the major theatre in the land of Kinraddie and the Guthrie clan.

His Majesty's Theatre in Aberdeen was opened in 1906 with a seating capacity at that time of over 2000, although that was subsequently reduced during refurbishment to just less than 1500. Built by Glasgow entrepreneur Robert Arthur, ownership was transferred to the Donald family in 1932. The Donald dynasty dominated the entertainment world in Aberdeen for a large part of the 20th century operating a sizable number of cinemas stretching from Torry to Kittybewster, and most points in between, with their two flagship picture houses, the Majestic and the Capitol, sited on a prestigious section of Union Street in the heart of the city. To reduce costs the company would often show the same film at different cinemas under their control at alternative times of the day with one of the younger members of the Donald clan tasked with cycling from one picture house to another carrying the film reels.

A second generation member of the family, Dick Donald, went on to enjoy great success in a very different field of entertainment as chairman of Aberdeen Football Club during the glory years of the Eighties when the team was managed by Sir Alex Ferguson. Devoted Dons' fans will always remember the witty banner carried by one member of the Red Army to Gothenburg on 11 May 1983 which read *'Gordon Strachan gives out more majestic passes than Dick Donald'*.

In 1975 Aberdeen City Council took over the running of HMT during an era which definitely couldn't boast the epithet 'glory', the theatre surviving on a diet of productions by local amateur companies and second rate touring productions, usually boasting actors in their twilight years. During these nights the theatre was generally sparsely filled and, having been heavily 'papered', few of those occupying a seat would actually have paid for a ticket.

The arrival of new artistic director by the name of Duncan Hendry, however, changed all that as he began to attract first rate shows that had genuinely served their apprenticeship in the London West End. But that wasn't enough for Duncan. Despite being Scotland's largest theatre out with Edinburgh and Glasgow it had got into the habit of always importing, never producing anything more than the seasonal pantomime. That was particularly embarrassing when seventy miles down the road the Dundee Rep, with less than a third of HMT's capacity, not only regularly produced new works which often toured the country but even employed its own full time company of actors.

Hendry decided to do something about that state of affairs and in 2008 Aberdeen Performing Arts, who had taken over running of the venue from the council, at last staged its own show. And for that significant occasion Hendry went back to Scotland's favourite book. The subsequent play proved to be a commercial hit but artistically didn't quite hit the heights.

A decision was made to put Paisley born actor/ director Kenny Ireland, best known for playing the obese character of Donald Stewart in TV's *Benidorm,* in charge and he travelled north with a band of West of Scotland actors drawn from the pool of regular establishment veterans some of whom encountered difficulties in mastering the local accent. Even the inclusion of a token Aberdonian merely highlighted the stark contrast between the guttural sounds of Torry and the soft languid tones of the Mearns. Some of the cast also struggled with the task of appearing as different characters with a change of costume being insufficient to convince the audience, leading to a slightly muddled telling of the complex story.

Fortunately locals flocked in droves to witness a genuine Aberdeen production and thanks to lucrative box office returns, Duncan Hendry was able to repeat the experiment twice more with excellent adaptations of well know Scottish literary works in the form of *The Silver Darlings* and *The Cone Gatherers.*

Not that the Aberdeen theatre was finished with Grassic Gibbon's most famous work as in November 2014 a new version, jointly produced by the *Beacon Centre in Greenock* and *Sell a Door Theatre Company* finished a major Scottish tour with a run at HMT. Under the direction of Julie Ellen it was vibrant and moving and coherently told the tale of love and loss. Alan McHugh who appeared as John Guthrie was an honorary Aiberdein loon having starred in the annual HMT Panto from the time of Methuselah while Rebecca Elise brought the central role of Chris Guthrie to life. The cast also boasted the likes of Clare Waugh as Chris's downtrodden mother and the always excellent MacDuff born actor Fraser Sivewright.

In the light of its success on stage and the small screen it is hardly surprising that there had been talk for years of adapting the book for the cinema but it wasn't until 2015 that actually happened.

Despite its plethora of characters *Sunset Song* largely revolves around the life of one, Chris Guthrie, and so the casting of that role was clearly important. Strangely the producers brought on board a relatively unknown actress by the name of Agyness Dyen and one who hails from Manchester, no doubt leaving a host of young aspiring Scottish actresses scratching their heads as to why they were not chosen. Now it has to be said in fairness that Deyn copes with the accent well and is an adequate Guthrie. However she never quite brings the character fully to life and fails to trawl the depths of strength that Grassic Gibbon endows on his book's leading lady.

The casting otherwise is fine with Peter Mullan a suitably foreboding and brutal father figure; mind you looking back over the actor's other works like *The Magdalene Sisters, My Name is Joe* and *Young Adam* it is hardly surprising that he masters the humourless and downright evil John Guthrie effortlessly. The film also uses the countryside with its wide and unspoilt vistas as an additional character in a highly effective way.

Where the film falls down is with the direction of Terence Davies, best known for his adaption of Terence Rattigan's *The Deep Blue Sea.* A great deal happens in the novel, especially during the early chapters, and the director should have cherry picked what to include and what to disregard. Instead Davies chooses to dramatise every single event with the result that we get episode after countless episode, some lasting little more than a minute or two, meaning that the movie clops along like one of the Guthrie's shire horses with an injured hoof and totally loses any sense of flow. Davies also employs, with annoying regularity, a cinematic trick of panning from the actor round an otherwise empty room seemingly for no other reason than to show off some fancy new camera he must have got for his Christmas.

Chris (Agyness Dyen) and John Guthrie (Peter Mullan)

As a consequence of these directorial shortcomings what could have been the definitive telling of the story ends up as nothing more than an adequate movie to watch on a rainy afternoon when there is nothing else to do.

Buoyed by the acclaim that *Sunset Song* had enjoyed the writer, under the Lewis Grassic Gibbon pseudonym, returned to the North East a year later with *Cloud Howe*, this time set in the fictional parish of Seggat it continued the story of Chris Guthrie and her new husband the Reverend Robert Colquohoun telling their story against a backdrop of the 1920's including the traumas of living through the General Strike. Like its predecessor it focuses on the small mindedness of life in a little community where the chief currency was gossip. It also brought to the fore Chris's son Ewan whose views on life are, too say the least, somewhat earthy.

Move forward another year to 1934 and *A Scots Quair* is complete with the publication of the final part of the trilogy, *Grey Granite*. As the title might suggest it is the toughest read and somewhat devoid of warmth, no doubt a deliberate ploy on the part of the writer who has moved Chris and her son away from the land that they know and love and dumped them down in the bleak setting of the industrial town of Duncairn at the height of the thirties Great Depression. The author's left wing leanings, having previously been a member of the British Socialist Party himself, hinted at in the earlier books begin to take centre stage and the upsurge in support for the Communist ideal surfaces.

All three books have become literary classics, loved the world over although initially not in the Mearns. Perhaps Grassic Gibbon fell into the same trap as his contemporary, Strichen born Lorna Moon whose book about the fictional Buchan village of Drumorty (*Doorways in Drumorty)* was banned for over 50 years in the local library in the town of her birth because locals recognised themselves and weren't best pleased how they were portrayed.

It is, however, more likely that in the case of the Grassic Gibbon books it was the subject matter rather than the characters that caused greatest offence. Suicide and a soldier shot for desertion were not subjects that the folk in the Mearns wanted to read about and many families refused to have the book in their houses while it is rumoured that when Mitchell returned home after the publication of *Sunset Song* that his father refused to shake his hand.

But above all it was the sexual element of the work including the father's efforts to convince his daughter to engage in incest that truly horrified the community; they knew that such things went on but they preferred for them to remain hidden behind the lace screens and just didn't want to talk or read about them. By the standards of the 21st century the content of the books would appear to be rather tame – they certainly weren't a *'Fifty Shades of Grey Granite'* – but for people raised in strict Presbyterian households and fed literature of the Mills and Boon variety they were undoubtedly rather racy and rather shocking.

1933 proved to be a remarkable year for the writer. Not only did he see *Cloud Howe* published but a second book reached the shelves with Mitchell trading Arbuthnot for Ancient Rome. Despite two thousand years having passed names like Caesar, Claudius, Caligula and Spartacus remain known to this day but what is extraordinary is that while the first three all attainted the role of Emperor of Rome the last named was never more than a slave.

Spartacus was born in what is now known as Bulgaria and became a Gladiator before leading a slaves' revolt in the Third Servile War in which he is thought to have been killed. In revenge for that uprising by the downtrodden the Romans crucified 6000 captured slaves along the Appan Way. The story of Spartacus is told in impressive style by director Stanley Kubbrick in his 1960 movie of the same name with Kirk Douglas taking the eponymous role and includes one of the most iconic, and plagiarised, scenes in film history in the form of 'I am Spartacus'. Sadly the 21st Century remake as a television series was little more than a gory mess of gratuitous violence, sex and cartoonish CGI.

Because of the cinematic adaptations people are now well aware of the Spartacus legend but the same was not true in the 1930's when Mitchell turned his attention to the subject matter. The resultant book was well received and reviewed and remains his most famous work out with the North East trilogy. What encouraged the writer to turn his attention to a subject so far removed from the novels for which he had become famous is difficult to tell although a clue may lie in his political affiliations as Karl Marx regarded Spartacus as one of his heroes. Indeed to this day there are numerous sporting clubs around Russia and other parts of the former Soviet Union whose names pay homage to the slave leader, the best known being FC Spartak Moscow.

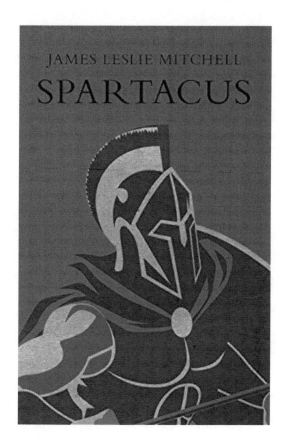

During the period from 1930 to 1934 Mitchell penned and had published under his own name and that of Grassic Gibbon no less than 16 novels and short stories, an astonishing output by any writer's standards. Near the end of that period he also became involved with another giant of the Scottish literary scene, Hugh MacDiarmid.

Like Mitchell, MacDiarmid was a pen name having been born on 11 August 1892 in Langholm in Dumfriesshire as Christopher Murray Grieve. With strong left wing tendencies he cut his teeth as a writer with the *Merthyr Pioneer,* a publication run by Keir Hardie, before heading back to his native Scotland where he took up a post as reporter with the *Montrose Review.* It was during that era that his books, largely comprising of a mixture of prose and poetry, began to be published. *Annals of the Five Senses* was followed by *Sangschaw* and *Penny Wheep,* before he produced his life's work. *A Drunk Man Looks at the Thistle* is a book-long poem, or linked series of poems, exploring many aspects of Scottish life from battles such as Bannockburn and Flodden to the General Strike of 1926 and incorporating such diverse figures as Robert Burns and dancer Isadora Duncan. To this day the work is remembered, revered and oft quoted.

Hugh MacDiarmid

After brief stays in London (working for Compton Mackenzie's magazine *Vox* magazine) followed by stints in Liverpool and Thakeham, MacDiarmid moved his family to the island of Whalsay in Shetland and settled in the interestingly named Sodom. Throughout his life he had strong political views being a founding member of the *National Party of Scotland*, the forerunner of the S.N.P., listing amongst his hobbies 'Anglophobia', although he was expelled from the party and subsequently enjoyed a brief dalliance with the Communist Party.

Throughout his long life, dying in Edinburgh in 1978 aged 86, he continued to write, almost exclusively in broad Scots. His involvement with Mitchell came courtesy of the *Scottish Scene* magazine to which Grassic Gibbon was invited to contribute three short stories, the best known of which was *Smeddum*. It is one of those wonderful Scottish words with no obvious English derivative and remains difficult to define. It could be described as determined or courageous or thrawn but in truth it is mixture of all three. That story along with two others, *Clay* and *Greenden* were dramatised by BBC's Play for Today in 1976.

During the later part of 1934 and while working on a new book to be titled *The Speak of the Mearns* (published posthumously in 1982) Mitchell began to suffer acute stomach pains but these were diagnosed as nothing more than gastritis. By February of the following year, however, his condition had deteriorated and he underwent an operation for a perforated ulcer at Queen Victoria Hospital in Welwyn Garden City but died on 7 February 1935 from Peritonitis. He was a month short of his 34th birthday. Fittingly he was buried in the small country church yard at Arbuthnott.

That is not, however, the end of the story as Mitchell's widow Rebecca, despite being left with two small children to raise on her own, laboured tirelessly throughout the remainder of her life to publicise her late husband's many works while the couple's daughter Rhea took over the task when her mother died in 1978. The opening of the Lewis Grassic Gibbon Centre at Arbuthnott in 1991 ensured that the flame was kept burning and the name and legacy would not be forgotten.

The Lewis Grassic Gibbon Centre at Arbuthnott

It is a delightful facility, comprising of an exhibition of photographs and memorabilia about the writer together with a book/ gift shop and a welcoming coffee shop. It is situated beside the Arbuthnott village hall which regularly plays host to music events and small scale theatre productions. The Centre is well worth a visit if only to step out after a hearty lunch to gaze over the tranquil Mearns vista that greets you. Close your eyes and you could almost visualise Chris Guthrie strolling through the fields of golden barley.

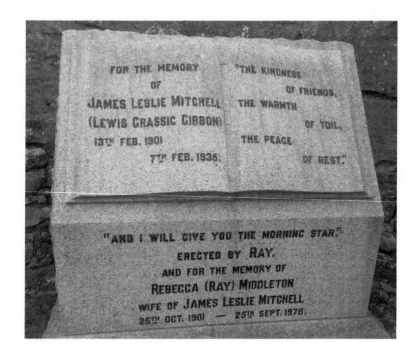

The gravestone in Arbuthnott cemetery for James Leslie and Rebecca Mitchell

Bill Gibb (1943-1988)

A sweet, sunny farm boy in baggy corduroys

The Daily Mail was first published in 1896 and throughout those 125 years they have stuck rigidly and faithfully to one maxim *'Never let the truth get in the way of a good story'*. They are, of course, not alone amongst tabloid newspapers in printing features with scant or no regard to the harm and offence they might cause but when it comes to attacks on anyone out with the realms of their ultra rightwing views the Daily Mail really has no equal.

On 3 January 1988 fashion designer Bill Gibb died aged just 44 leaving behind elderly grieving parents and siblings as well as a host of friends who loved and admired the gentle soul. Bill Gibb died of bowel cancer but clearly that made for a boring story so the Daily Mail opted for something much more eye catching suggesting that *'Fashion designer dies of Aids'*. The paper was in the midst of one of its self righteous tirades aimed to please the twin set and pearls Surbiton set, this one focusing on what they loved to refer to as the 'gay plague'. They clearly didn't bother checking with the London hospital where Bill had been treated but simply assumed that because he was young and a designer of ladies attire that it obviously must have been Aids that killed him. They could have used a quote from Twiggy as their headline describing Bill Gibb as *'a sweet, sunny farm boy in baggy corduroys whom I absolutely adored'* but that would have had two major disadvantages; it wasn't particularly sensational and it was true.

William Elphinstone Gibb, or Billy as his parents George and Jessie called him, was born on 23 January 1943 near New Pistligo, and being the eldest of a family of seven he spent a great deal of his youth with his grandparents at Lochpots farm, Fraserburgh. From an early age he loved drawing and sketching and was encouraged to do so by his grandmother who herself painted landscapes of which there was a profusion to be found around the farm house. Bill attended Fraserburgh Academy where he excelled in art so much so that his Art teacher, Bob Duthie, realising that the boy was exceptionally talented, encouraged him to go 'South'. Being a country loon Bill was reticent to move away from his native North East but a WRI prize changed that. He won the sum of £25 in a 'Rural' drawing competition and used the money to help finance a school trip to Rome. On the way he passed through London for the first time and was suitably impressed and anxious to return.

Bill with Isobel Gregory during their Fraserburgh Academy days

Months after arriving at Saint Martin's School of Art in London Bill wanted to do only one thing. Get back to the Broch. He was only nineteen and felt lonely and out of place, other students clearly having difficulty in understanding his accent. Although he enjoyed the scholastic work he missed his native North East of Scotland and throughout his life he would return whenever he could to walk the Aberdeenshire fields and beaches and enjoy his Mum's home cooking. But encouraged by his Gran he displayed grit and gradually settled into life at the chic college situated on Charing Cross Road right in the heart of London, an establishment that could later boast the likes of Bruce Oldfield and Pierce Brosnan amongst its alumni. It was also where the controversial punk band the Sex Pistols made their first appearance.

St Martin's School of Art

Sketchbooks which have survived from his later years at school clearly display his abilities and often depict, in meticulous detail, the fashions of the time. He quickly displayed those design talents at the College but struggled with the practical elements of making garments and it became clear to his parents the he was far from settled in either

London or at Saint Martin's. His Mum and Dad were so concerned that he might throw away this golden opportunity that they travelled to London to meet Muriel Pemberton, the Dean of the college. Following a subsequent heart to heart chat with Bill, she was able to convince him that if he stuck at it he would eventually master the process of making the clothes and he remained at the establishment repaying Ms. Pemberton's faith in him by graduating top of his class and, as a result, being awarded a scholarship to the Royal College of Art.

A selection of Bill's earliest fashion designs drawn when aged 15

The Royal College was a very different establishment with its chief campus being in the considerably more staid South Kensington. It also had an illustrious history of welcoming famous people from all disciplines of the arts through its doors and in 2020 it was voted number one in the world for art and design for the sixth year in a row. It was a great honour for the young lad from Fraserburgh to be invited to study there but Bill never graduated from the Royal College, attracted away from the academic establishment by the lure of the business world and even brighter lights

In 1967 the cosmetic and perfume manufacturer Yardleys invited six young designers to take part in their 'London Look' award scheme which involved them presenting their designs in New York City before embarking on a three month research tour of the USA. Their arrival in the Big Apple was greeted with curiosity and the leading fashion houses sent along representatives to see what the Bright Young Things, as Anna Godbersen might have described them, had to offer. And there amongst the voyeurs were senior staff members from the crème de la crème, Bendel's of Fifth Avenue.

Founded in 1895 by Henri Willis Bendel who had moved to New York from Louisiana it began with a modest store in Greenwich Village before moving to 712 Fifth Avenue. Bendels would eventually boast 23 stores in America although the last of these closed its doors for the final time in 2018. At its height, however, it was clearly one of the places for the rich and the famous to go to shop, and to be seen shopping, and was immortalised by Cole Porter in his song 'You're The Tops' with the lines *'you're a Bendels bonnet, a Shakespeare sonnet'*.

The rather shy Bill Gibb was clearly overawed and overwhelmed by the whole affair and the illustrious and worldly people he was mixing with but fortunately his designs spoke for themselves; they were greatly admired and Bendels commissioned the complete collection for their stores. On that trip to the States, Gibb was accompanied by a fellow artist and textile designer with who he was in a relationship and who remained a close friend and collaborator throughout his life. The man's name was Kaffe Fassett.

Bill Gibb with Kaffe Fassett in the Alice Paul Boutique

Fassett was born in San Francisco in 1937 and came from a well-to-do American family with his grandfather a State Senator and his great grandfather the founder of the Crocker Arts Museum in Sacramento. Kaffe followed along that same artistic road by attending the School of the Museum of Fine Arts in Boston but in 1964 he headed for London where he subsequently met Bill Gibb. Throughout Gibb's all too short life the two men worked together with Fassett often designing the complex multi coloured designs that became a trademark of Bill's clothes, in particular his knitwear.

Kaffe has gone on to become a world famous fashion designer with his own television show in the 1980's and numerous books published.

And yet he has continued to keep in close contact with Gibb's family inviting them to many retrospective of Bill's work and most of his own exhibitions, even treating the three Gibb sisters to dinner in London on one occasion to celebrate one of the ladies special birthdays. He also held a workshop in Tyrie primary school as well as opening the 'The Golden Boy of British Fashion' exhibition in 2003 at the Aberdeen Art Gallery on what would have been Bill's 60th birthday.

In the later part of the 1960's the group of would-be young designers returned from their tour of the States to a London in the grip of the 'Swinging Sixties'. The name was derived from a cover article in an edition of Time magazine from April 1966 with the headline 'The Swinging City' and was driven by a youth movement enjoying the sexual revolution and becoming politically active through the anti-nuclear movement. Music was hugely important with bands like The Small Faces, The Rolling Stones, The Kinks and The Who enjoying great success as a consequence of the emergence of pirate radio stations providing a welcome alternative to the sedate and boring BBC.

At the heart of the Swinging Sixties was undoubtedly fashion with trendy clothes shops popping up all over London but in particular on Chelsea's Kings Road and Kensington High Street, with its flagship store Biba, and yet the place to go during that era was undoubtedly Carnaby Street. Although a number of Gentlemen's outfitters had opened there in the fifties it was little more than a back street in Soho overshadowed by the nearby bustling retail thoroughfares of Regent Street and Oxford Street until shops like Mary Quant and basement music clubs opened and it became the place to go and to be seen. It was against this London backdrop that Bill and a few friends founded the Alice Paul boutique with Gibb designing miniskirts and long coats, popular fashion items in the later part of the decade, while his friends attended to manufacturing and marketing. Around that time

Bill also began doing freelance design work for a fashion house called Baccarat.

Bill Gibb with Nives Losani his long time collaborator/ seamstress

That proved to be a match made in heaven and a year after he had begun working with Baccarat, Vogue magazine chose an outfit designed by Bill Gibb as their 'Dress of the Year' as did the Bath Fashion Museum. It was a pleated tartan skirt with a printed blouse married to a Kaffe Fassett knitted waistcoat. This accolade not only put Gibb firmly in the limelight but also changed the world of fashion by making traditional designs involving hand knitted items and the use of tartan acceptable in the world of contemporary fashion. The durability of Bill's work is displayed by the online site Etsy, an American website along the lines of the better known Ebay but specialising in handmade or vintage items. To this day items of Baccarat clothing, described as being 'designed by Bill Gibb' are offered for sale and often at prices that would require potential purchasers to have deep pockets. A Kaftan dress recently sold for £1500.

By 1970 Bill was voted 'Designer of the Year' by Vogue magazine, an important moment for him in many ways including the fact that he wouldn't have to adhere to the vow he had made to his Mum that 'if I don't make it by age 30 I will be back to drive Dad's tractor'. Buoyed by the success he was enjoying he launched his own company the 'Bill Gibb Fashion Group' in 1972, with many of the garments he made being adorned with an image of a bee which quickly became his trademark. Three years later he opened his first shop on Bond Street. But a store on that prestigious West London Boulevard didn't quite compare with the arrival of the 'Bill Gibb Room' as that particular 'Room' was to be found in what is arguably the most famous shop in the world. Harrods.

Born in Colchester at the very end of the 18th century, Charles Henry Harrod worked as a miller in Clacton before moving to London aged

25, establishing 'Harrod & Wicking, Linen Drapers, Retail' in Southwark. In the following years he set up grocery businesses firstly in Clerkenwell and then Stepney although doing so wasn't always plain sailing. The Police had long suspected him of receiving stolen goods working in association with Richard Moran, a porter at rival grocers Booth, Ingledew and Co., and in 1836 they were able to prove that Harrod had illegally taken in 112 lbs. of currants. He was arrested for receiving stolen goods with a value of £3 5s and both Moran and Harrod were found guilty and sentenced to deportation to Tasmania for seven years.

Harrods in the late 19th Century

In a desperate effort to avoid that fate a petition was submitted to the King on Harrod's behalf begging for clemency on the grounds that he had '*a wife and two children, the elder only three and half and the younger a little more than a year, both, as well as his unfortunate partner, in delicate health, and threatened with the most unfortunate consequences should your unhappy petitioner be removed from this country for a term of seven years*'.

It worked as his sentence was reduced to a year in an English jail while poor Mr. Moran ended up on the boat headed down under. During his year at His Majesty's pleasure the business was looked after by his brother William before Charles returned to take over the reins.

In 1851 the Great Exhibition was to be held in Hyde Park and Harrod decided to capitalise on the vastly increased footfall in the Knightsbridge area of London by opening a small store on Brompton Road. The shop was subsequently taken over by the founder's son Charles Digby Harrod and over the course of many years he built up the business diversifying into the sale of the likes of perfumes, stationery and medicines. Thirty years after the shop had opened, adjacent properties having been purchased and developed, the business was employing over 100 people.

But misfortune struck in December 1883 when fire broke out and the property was totally destroyed. Determined not to let down customers in the run up to Christmas Harrod acquired alternate premises and succeeded in fulfilling every order making a record profit in the process. The property was rebuilt on the original site but bigger and grander than before and having introduced charge accounts Harrods were able to boast a highly impressive stable of celebrated customers that included the likes of Oscar Wilde, Charlie Chaplin, Laurence Olivier, A.A. Milne, Sigmund Freud and many others together with several residents of Buckingham Palace.

Unfortunately the second Mr. Harrod was the last of that name with a hand on the tiller. A chance meeting with a London businessman by the name of Edgar Cohen resulted in Charles Digby Harrod bowing out with the sum of £120,000 in his pocket. Fortunately the new owner had no wish to lose the esteemed name and formed Harrod Stores Ltd. One of the first changes was the installing of the country's first 'moving staircase', now better known as an escalator. Customers were initially reluctant to use it and a member of staff was positioned at the top of the stairway to proffer glasses of brandy to those brave enough to utilise it in order to help them to recover from the ordeal.

Ownership of the store passed to the House of Fraser in 1959 and consequently came under the umbrella of the Fayed Brothers. In 2010 rumours began to circulate that Mohamed Al-Fayed was contemplating selling the business with interest coming from a number of wealthy Middle Eastern countries. In response Fayed declared '*People approach us from Kuwait, Saudi Arabia, Qatar. Fair enough. But I put two fingers up to them. It is not for sale. This is not Marks and Spencer or Sainsbury's. It is a special place that gives people pleasure. There is only one Mecca.*' Two weeks later he sold it to the ruling family of Qatar.

Despite the changes of ownership Harrods can still call itself the finest departmental store in the world and it must have been a great boost to the young fashion designer when a room named after him was opened there. It was during that same era that a young lady entered his life and elevated him from cult status to universal recognition. The girl's name was Lesley Hornby but she became rather better known as Twiggy.

Lesley was born on 19 September 1949 in Neasden in Middlesex and was taught how to sew by her mother resulting in her being able make her own clothes. In early 1966, aged just sixteen, she went to Leonards of Mayfair, a fashionable hairdressing salon as the owner was looking for models to try out a new crop hair style. Lesley volunteered to not only have her hair cut in that manner but to have a series of photographs subsequently put on display in the salon.

Deirdre McSharry, a fashion journalist with the Daily Express, saw the photos, asked to meet the young girl and months later Lesley was on the cover of the newspaper, described as 'the face of 1966'. Her career as a model instantly took off and copying the style of her great heroine Jean Shrimpton she was soon in great demand. Her boyfriend at the time was a hairdresser called Nigel Davies who became her manager after changing his name to the rather more exotic Justin De Villeneuve and he persuaded Lesley to adopt the moniker Twiggy, appropriate because of her ultra slim figure.

Twiggy and Justin visiting the Gibbs with their dog which ate some of the farm's chickens

Within a year Twiggy was featured on the cover of Vogue and Tatler magazines and began a period of several years when she was in great demand as a model around the world with her arrival at Kennedy Airport in New York creating media frenzy. Her meteoric rise to fame was best highlighted by the fact that in December 1969 she was chosen as the subject of the TV programme 'This Is Your Life'. She was 20 years old.

By the time she had turned twenty one she had largely given up modelling and was perusing other career paths. She became friendly with maverick film Director Ken Russell and after a bit part in *The Devils* she was cast in the lead role of Polly Browne in a movie adaption of the stage musical *The Boyfriend*. Written by Sandy Wilson as a pastiche of 1920's musicals, the original stage version provided Julie Andrews with her first major role.

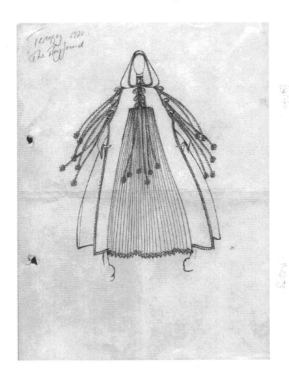

Sketch of the dress Bill designed for Twiggy for *The Boyfriend* premiere in 1971

The film netted Twiggy two Golden Globe Awards as *Best Actress in a Musical or Comedy* and *New Star of the Year*. She also began what became a rather intermittent singing career and took to the London stage in *Cinderella* before making a second film simply called *W* starring opposite American actor Michael Witney. The couple wed in 1977 and Twiggy gave birth to a daughter Carly two years later.

Tragically the couple were married for only six years with Whitney dying from a heart attack, aged 52, in 1983.

Twiggy in a Bill Gibb creation

Twiggy's varied career continued to flourish and she received a Tony nomination for her Broadway debut in *My One and Only,* a rather lightweight stage confection developed from an old Gershwin song of the same title. During the eighties and nineties she made regular stage appearances on both sides of the Atlantic, acted in a number of films and turned up in a wide variety of TV shows. Not many people can boast having been on both *The Muppet Show* and *Absolutely Fabulous*.

Married to English actor Leigh Lawson she began to reduce her workload and although recently she became involved with the likes of Marks & Spencer she is now devoting a great deal of her time to various charities that support breast cancer research, anti-fur campaigns and animal welfare issues. In the 2019 New Year's Honours list she was made a Dame under the name of Lesley Lawson.

It was when Bill was still a young and struggling designer that he first met Twiggy and a friendship was formed that lasted throughout his life. In 1970 Twiggy attended the Daily Mirror's Fashion Celebrity Dinner and as a huge boost to Bill wore a dress designed by him. But the following year there was an even more prestigious evening when *The Boyfriend* film premiered and its star turned up in a gown, made from a number of different patterned materials, bearing Gibb's signature bee motif, designed and made by her new pal.

The famous Bill Gibb motif

This brought Bill to a much wider audience and he was suddenly in demand to 'dress' the likes of Joan Collins and Elizabeth Taylor. The latter would ask him to visit her in her suite at the Dorchester Hotel with samples of his work some of which she would reject because they were for 'skinny women'. On one occasion Bill must have been slightly bemused when he saw Liz Taylor in a dress he had made for her being worn back to front only to be informed that she deliberately wore it that way as it better displayed her cleavage.

Mr. Bill Gibb.

Hosts
DR. & MRS. ZEV BUFMAN
MR. LOUIS BENJAMIN, M.B.E.

Supper Party
honouring
Elizabeth Taylor
AND THE CAST
of
LITTLE FOXES
Gala Premier Performance
»
LANCASTER ROOM
»
Thursday 11th March 1982

Invitation to a Supper Party at the Savoy with Elizabeth Taylor

Another celebrity that was a huge fan of his designs was Bianca Jagger, wife of the Rolling Stones lead singer, who many years after Bill had passed away maintained a packed wardrobe of Bill Gibb clothes. The uniqueness of his clothes was best summed up by Ann Chubb of the Daily Telegraph who wrote in the newspaper '*only someone who has actually owned a Bill Gibb knit can appreciate the gap it fills in a wardrobe*'.

But it wasn't just international celebrities that Bill designed for as his three sisters, Patsy, Janet and Marlyn were married in his creations. The first of these was Patricia (Patsy) who travelled to London to choose material and regular calls asking to see sketches of what Bill had in mind went unheeded and she was forced to trust her brother. Indeed the first inkling of what her brother had in mind for her was revealed only on the eve of the wedding when Bill and his faithful seamstress Nives Losani arrived with their creation although pearls were still being added. Even on the wedding day there was a last minute addition with Nives insisting they followed an Italian tradition of sewing strands of horse hair into the hem to bring good luck and Bill's father was dispatched to cut the mane of one of his beloved horses.

Wedding and Bridesmaid dresses designed by Bill for his sisters

Her sister Marlyn had a similar experience as after flying to London and expecting to try on a dress, she discovered that Bill was not at home and when he did eventually appear she found that the 'dress' was little more than a few pieces of material which were then pinned onto her with the reassuring words 'it will be lovely'. Fortunately she totally trusted her hugely talented sibling and the finished article, topped off by a headdress made at 5am on the day of the wedding, made her feel like a 'million dollars'.

A year after *The Boyfriend* movie premiere Bill presented a collection under his own name having worked tirelessly seven days a week for three months to get it ready. In 1972 he returned to his native North East and for once not just to chill out down on the farm but for a fashion show at the Royal Darroch Hotel in Cults which all the family attended. His sister Patsy is not sure that the people of Aberdeen were quite ready back then for Bill's inventive and at times atypical creations.

Bill at the Royal Darroch Hotel with family and models

As the demand for his clothes continued to grow a problem arose; the designs were intricate and often involved a use of fur, feathers and leather and a wide variety of vibrant colours. His long time collaborator Mildred Boulton continued to produce one-off items to meet specific demands but it was clear with the expanding business that manufacture on a larger scale was essential. Several companies were unable to cope with the complexities of the patterns and it was only when Gibb came across a company called Goulds of Leicester, who were able to achieve what he wanted, that that particular problem was solved. As a result Gibb found himself in a position where he could diversify still further.

H. & M. Rayne was founded in 1899 by Henry and Mary Rayne, setting up as theatrical costumiers in premises close to the Old Vic Theatre in Lambeth. Early clients included famed ballet stars Anna Pavlova and Vaslav Nijinsky. Although it was not their forte at the time they received a request to produce shoes for actress Lillie Langtry and as it emanated from King Edward VII, with whom Langtry was having an affair, they buckled down and got on with the task.

By 1920 they decided that there was a future in producing quality shoes and with a Royal warrant secured the business flourished from a shop in fashionable New Bond Street. Queen Elizabeth II, Princess Margaret and Princess Anne all wore Rayne shoes on their wedding day as did Elizabeth Taylor in the title role of the film *Cleopatra*. In

1952 Edward Rayne, grandson of the original owners, took over the business and expanded it internationally as a result of which they attracted a client roster that included the likes of Ava Gardner, Rita Hayworth, Vivien Leigh and Brigitte Bardot.

In 1975 the business was sold to Debenhams, rather a climb down from its dizzy heights, but was 'rescued' in 1987 by businessman David Graham and his wife Rose who ran it until it ceased trading in 2003. But that wasn't the end of the Rayne brand as ten years later it rose once again and, with designer Laurence Dacade on board, the Rayne name was not only restored but flourishes to this day.

It was quite a feather in Bill Gibb's cap when the young man was approached to create Rayne shoes bearing in mind the previous designers that the company had worked with included the likes of Mary Quant and Norman Hartnell.

As the 70's progressed all must have seemed rosy in the Gibb garden with show after successful show, even filling the Royal Albert Hall to its 7000 capacity for a 10 year retrospective exhibition of his work in 1977. It is an event which his sister Patsy still remembers with great affection especially when her brother was dragged onto the catwalk at the end to be greeted by a standing ovation. She found it hard to believe that it was 'oor Billy' that everyone was enthusiastically applauding. Unfortunately he put so much heart and soul and talent into designing and making the outfits for the shows that when they were over he was left drained and depressed.

Another problem he encountered arose from the fact that although he was artistically talented he had little head for commerce, admitting that he was naive when it came to the profit side of the business. There was real concern that the company had grown too fast and in the later part of that decade the business collapsed on more than one occasion. As the eighties came along he had re-established himself by largely designing for individual clients and producing small scale collections. He also teamed up with the UK magazine *Women's*

Journal offering ensembles to readers on a mail order basis. Back on a firmer financial footing, in 1985 he launched a new 'Bronze Age' collection working with his long time friend and collaborator Kaffe Fassett. Sadly it failed to attract the buying public in sufficient numbers to make it financially viable.

By the late eighties his health was causing alarm and he was diagnosed with bowel cancer, undergoing an operation which proved unsuccessful. In December 1987 he was admitted to St. Stephen's Hospital in Fulham and as the New Year arrived Bill had slipped into a coma. On 3 January 1988, less than three weeks short of his forty fifth birthday, Bill Gibb died with his devoted family at his bedside.

Selection of Bill Gibb creations at 'Moment in Time' exhibition

He was gone but certainly not forgotten with modern day designers like John Galliano and Giles Deacon declaring how influenced they had been by Gibb's work and with facilities like the Bath Fashion Museum and Fashion and Textile Museum in the Bermondsey holding one-off exhibitions of his work. His legacy is also remembered for perpetuity by the exalted Victoria and Albert Museum which has permanent collections of his work on display in both their London and Dundee Museums as have the Metropolitan Museum of Art in New York, the Manchester City Galleries and the Walker Art Gallery in Liverpool.

One of the most important events to cement Bill's legacy occurred in October 2008 when an exhibition called 'Moment in Time' opened at the Fashion and Textile Museum in London. Covering two floors of the building it displayed 60 of Bill's creations covering the best part of two decades. The exhibition was opened by Twiggy and hosted by Zandra Rhodes and it was remarkable just how many of the celebrities who attended the opening night were wearing Bill Gibb clothes.

Exhibition in the Fraserburgh Heritage Centre

There is also a permanent exhibit about Bill in the Fraserburgh Heritage Centre a facility that received £888 when an item given to Bill in 1978 was put up for auction. It was a silver disc for the album 'Love's a Prima Donna' by Steve Harley and Cockney Rebel which the singer had given to Bill, adding a personal note saying 'if clothes maketh the man, Bill Gibb helped to make me'.

Fifteen years after his death the Aberdeen Art Gallery staged a hugely successful retrospective event drawing from the collection of 120 of his garments and 2500 of his sketches and drawings in their possession while in February 2020 the recently refurbished gallery staged an exhibition called 'The Bill Gibb Line'.

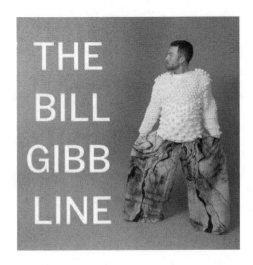

It was created by a fellow Brocher, Aberdeen based writer-performer Shane Strachan who became interested in Bill Gibb after visiting the Heritage Centre and researching the man's work while studying for a PhD. at University. Shane initially intended producing a book about the designer but instead wrote a number of poems focusing on different fashion shows which was then developed into a short film with Shane performing six of the poems. An extract from one written to mark Bill's exhibition at Aberdeen Cowdray Hall in October 1977, which concentrates on the Scottish influences on the designer's work, is reproduced below.

This season Gibb is serving Scotch on the frocks

with sensual fur bodices and soft lacy shirts

that give tartan the sort of p.m. panache

Bonnie Prince Charlie would fail to match.

Billy bows to royalty by embroidering

thistles and roses on almost everything,

from velvets that spice up subdued tartan skirts

to worsted panels on fabulous fox coats.

A beacon for British fashion, Gibb was greeted

with aching handclaps and echoing whoops

for this bold return to his native roots.

The Aberdeen Art Gallery event combined the video with a display of original garments and sketches and new clothes produced by students of Gray's School of Art and inspired by the late designer. Shane also produced a fascinating one hour podcast, telling Bill's story in his own words, and gave an online talk to the V & A Dundee about Gibb.

Bearing in mind that Bill's talent was noticed at Fraserburgh Academy it is indeed fitting that in 2010 the family should create a Bill Gibb Award presented, on the first occasion by Bill's Mum, to a student of the school who displayed a real passion for the arts while a Bill Gibb Resource pack was distributed to every school, both primary and secondary, through Aberdeenshire.

Gibb is not only remembered as a unique talent but also a thoroughly decent man who worked in a highly competitive and, on occasions, rather bitchy field of endeavour. North East journalist and writer Jack Webster described him as '*one of the most gentle, kindly and considerate human beings I have ever met – a man without malice'*.

But it is only fitting that the final word should be given to Twiggy, a woman who helped put Bill firmly in the spotlight and, in the process, became a dear friend.

'*Bill Gibb was my friend and I loved him. He was also one of the great fashion designers of the 20th century.*

We met by chance one very snowy day in London in the late 1960's. I came down from my flat, in Notting Hill, one morning to find my car, a Mini, completely snowed in and I didn't know how I was going to get it out of the snow drift, when this man came towards me and said in a lovely, soft Scottish accent, "Can I help?" He then proceeded to dig my car out of the snow. It turned out that he lived a few doors along the road. So he invited me in for a hot cup of tea. My knight in shining armour was Bill. I loved him immediately and we became close friends from that day on. He also made me some of the most beautiful clothes. He was so talented, his designs were gorgeous and very romantic. I think there are still a couple of the outfits he made for me in the Victoria & Albert Museum in London. When I did a series of concerts in the 1970's, finishing at the Royal Albert Hall, he made me the most beautiful costumes, which I am happy to say I still have.

We lost this sweet, gentle, talented man far too soon, and I will always miss him'.

Dame Twiggy Lawson, DBE

The Companion book *Forgotten Heroines of the North East* focuses on operas singer Mary Garden, International Brigade nurse Annie Murray, missionary Mary Slessor, scientist and suffrage supporter Maia Ogilvie Gordon and Hollywood screenplay writer and author Lorna Moon.

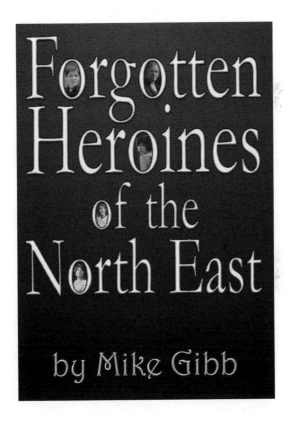

The book is available for £5.99 plus postage by contacting author Mike Gibb at <ins>mikegibb32@outlook.com</ins> or on 07903 463163. Books come signed and with a dedication of choice. All proceeds will be donated to the Bianca animal rescue centre in Sesimbra, Portugal.